ONE *Equals Six*

This book is dedicated to all the special needs parents who are doing it all alone. And especially the real “Dianna” and “Alicia” for whom I send all the love and yellow butterflies. I love you.

You can write your story too.
www.facebook.com/SprayBooksEtc
www.michellespray.com

One Equals Six
by Michelle Spray ©2021

Published by
Book Shelf
1083 East Main St.
Suite C4, PMB 111
Torrington, CT 06790
www.michellespray.com

Editor: Natalie Bates
Cover Photo: © Michelle Spray 2021
Cover Design: © Michelle Spray 2021

ISBN: 978-0-578-92100-6

-1-

Faith clutched the steering wheel, peering into the playground. Jenna had behaved at her brother's doctor's appointment and Faith knew the rest of the day would run smoother if she allowed Jenna to run off some toddler energy. She also knew that once Jenna saw where they were, there was no turning back.

"Mama. In." Jenna pestered.

Faith examined her bloodshot eyes in the driver's side mirror. "We can go in, but we have to get home to clean before your father gets home. Five times down the slide."

"More times." Jenna suggested, already too smart.

"Ten," Faith said, although she knew she wouldn't actually be counting. She mustered the energy to get herself out of the car, unbuckle Jenna and lug Kyle's baby seat from the cradle. She watched Jenna run off, her blonde curls bouncing with each skip.

"Mama, watch," she insisted.

"Great job honey," Faith said, cursing the mulch that lodged in the wheels of Kyle's stroller, nearly toppling him over. She headed toward the bench under the shade of her favorite maple, reading the inscription for the thousandth time: *"Change. Fly. Soar."* She ran her hand over the ornate letter "A" engraved along the back. She looked up and smiled before resting against the etched butterflies, scents of honeysuckle and fresh cut grass swirled past her. Sometimes Faith picked the dried leaves and plastic straws out from between the thorns of the rosebush, but on this day she sat and practiced her deep breathing, willing relaxation to come even though she was well aware of the time.

Experience taught her she'd have to give Jenna plenty of time to resist leaving. Ah, the terrible twos. Months earlier before Kyle was born, Faith had taken a day off from work to spend a Mommy-and-Me day with Jenna at the zoo. "No walk mama." Jenna rolled on the ground having a tantrum. Faith scooped her up while people stared at the crazy woman forcing a deprived child to leave the zoo within minutes of their arrival. Sweat poured down her face and puddled between her breasts. Her belly stretched to the max and with a bladder about to burst, she crossed the expanse of scorching pavement, hysterical child under her arm. By the time she made it to the car, surely she'd either peed herself or her water had broken because she was completely soaked. After settling Jenna in her car seat, Faith had taken a deep breath behind the wheel, gaining the composure to head home.

Faith jumped when Jenna appeared in front of her at the bench, dropping her hands in her lap. "Mama?"

"Yes, honey, Mama's fine. Good girl for coming without Mommy having to call you." Faith looked at the time on her phone. She knew to the millisecond how long it took to get home and prepare for dinner. "Did you count how many times you went down the slide?"

Faith sped home and rushed through the house,

handing Jenna the snack she'd demanded, tossing as many toys as possible into the bins around the perimeter of the living room before Frank came home. The house *should* have been sparkling, dinner ready and waiting, the last thing she needed was for him to remind her. Faith's heart pounded. She picked up the pace. No need to start a fight unnecessarily. "Clean and calm," she thought. She glanced around the room, the new carpet had recently been installed, so there was no reason for a mess. She did nothing all day, you know? Or at least that's what Frank told her. She caught a whiff of something less than fragrant though and winced until she found the culprit. "I thought that thing was supposed to trap odors." She glanced at the latch on the diaper bucket. "Or … is that me?" She sniffed inside her shirt and winced. Worry-free showers were luxuries. She couldn't find a few minutes to herself without someone needing her.

Kyle settled in easily for a nap for the moment. Faith resisted the urge to snuggle her face into his plush pajamas. Instead she watched for the slight rise and fall of his chest and tiptoed out of the room. She poured yesterday's leftovers into a skillet when Jenna shrieked from the toilet. Tossing the place settings in a heap on the table, Faith turned the burner off and ran toward the bathroom. She knelt next to the toilet and began rubbing Jenna's legs. She praised her for going on the potty all by herself. Jenna's groans increased with each push, startling Kyle who had never awoken peacefully, ever.

Faith started to go to him. "No go Mama," Jenna pleaded. Kyle's reflux made him scream out in the perfect mixture of colic and pain, sounding horrific to any stranger passing by. But she knew he'd be okay for a few minutes. She'd have plenty of time to take care of Jenna first and comfort Kyle before Frank barged in.

"What the hell are you doing?" Frank startled Jenna who started crying and Kyle ramped up, getting more agitated. "The baby's screaming."

"I know that." Faith pulled some toilet paper off the roll in anticipation of Jenna needing help.

"Are you doing anything about it?" Frank badgered.

Faith twisted a piece of toilet paper until it crumbled into tiny pieces in her hand. "I'm a little busy here." Jenna's legs shook, her face strained from pushing. "It's okay honey. Stay calm. It will feel better soon."

Frank waved his arms toward Kyle's room, not making sense, barricading them in the bathroom.

"Frank. What is wrong with you?" She dislodged herself from between him and the toilet, stepping closer to inspect him. He stumbled back. "It's not even 5:30! You were … at work?" She questioned.

"Don't worry about it." His words slurred.

Her mouth dropped. "Unreal. Go. Get your son." She pointed down the hall.

"I don't … know how." He stood and stared.

"For God's sake! Pick him up. Make him a bottle."

"Why can't you do it?" He mumbled.

"Oh com' on. Help me for once. Can you see I need help? I can't do it all by myself. You need to help me." Faith's voice quivered.

"What are you going to cry now too?"

"Frank, this is ridiculous."

"So I'm the problem?"

Faith clenched her fist and inhaled before pushing past him. "Move."

"Mama no go. Stay wid me. Dada go." Her tiny voice, more baby-like in the moment.

"Frank, Please. Go get Kyle."

"I can't. I don't know what's wrong."

"Just pick him up, he's probably hungry again, like usual." Kyle only ever ate two ounces every hour if they were lucky. "Get him a bottle. You know how to make it. But be sure to feed him sitting up so it doesn't spew everywhere." She rolled her eyes, tired of explaining.

"I'll stay with Jenna."

"No Dada, Mama only." Jenna whined.

Frank left the room in a huff to make the bottle, Faith hoped.

Jenna started to calm down when her belly felt better.

"See, I told you it would be okay." Faith dabbed Jenna's face with a washcloth, instructing her to wash her hands. When Faith got to Kyle's crib, Frank was standing over him in a trance. She shoved him out of the way, hard. For a brief second she fantasized about pushing him all the way through the closed window. She picked up Kyle, kissing his hot face, making hushing sounds in his ear to calm him, leaving Frank in the room staring at the empty crib.

Faith struggled to make the bottle with one hand while rocking Kyle in the other arm. But it didn't help; he was beyond comforting. She hoped he wasn't getting sick again. The poor child always seemed to get getting sick. He did stop as soon as the milk hit his mouth though and Faith paced with him from room to room. "Jenna, honey, get a book and a blanket. Do you want to cuddle up with Mama and help me feed Kyle?"

Jenna spun around like a top, squealing. Helping with

Kyle's feeding was one of her favorite things.

Frank brushed past them.

"Where are you going?"

"Out."

"Out where? You just got home."

"Well, obviously you didn't make dinner."

"Hello? It's on the stove."

"We had that last night."

"You can help cook too you know. Or buy it. Pick up a pizza once in a while."

"I work."

"You're an accountant, not a brain surgeon."

"You're on maternity leave. That means you're home all day not working. And this place is a pig-sty." Frank continued out the door.

"I swear Frank, if you leave … it's over."

"Riiight. You've said that before." He slammed the door behind him. Faith froze, staring at the shut door to the outside world; the world of freedom; of no responsibilities.

"Sure, go," she screamed. "Walk out the door." You know I'll just take you back like I always do. But why? Why is that okay? Faith cursed herself for letting it happen. She imagined changing the locks on the door and Frank begging to come in when she felt Kyle's body tense and all the milk he just drank spewed out of his nose into the tarp she had ready.

"Dad go?" Jenna asked.

"He'll be back."

"I make dad mad?"

"You? Oh, no honey, not you." Faith pushed down the anger that had bubbled up and faked a smile. "No, honey, come here!" Faith planted a dozen kisses all over Jenna's soft face and looked her in the eye. "It's never your fault." Faith swallowed a lump in her throat. "Daddy was … having a bad day."

Jenna giggled when Faith found her ticklish spot. "I la uooo Mama. I la uooo 'Brudder'," Jenna kissed Kyle on the forehead. *I love you; the most perfect phrase in the world.* Faith couldn't bear to correct her pronunciation.

"I love you too Honey Bunches." Faith scooped her up in her other arm and headed to the kitchen to clean up the mess and put the leftovers back. They wouldn't be eating together as a family tonight, again. She sliced up some bananas while Jenna's buttered pasta warmed. Faith ate pasta with Jenna instead of the leftovers that were in the pan on the stove. Typically if Faith anticipated that Frank was having a rough night, she would send the kids to bed early so she wouldn't have to introduce them to the terms 'slurring' and 'staggering'. But baths, books, and tummy time first, which Kyle despised. He didn't have the strength to lift his head. Milestones? Crawling? Holding his own bottle? None of that was on the horizon, yet.

Jenna enjoyed singing into the toy microphone or dancing to get the sillies out. She could only do this when Frank wasn't home because it wasn't exactly the quietest toy. Plus, she had to be reminded not to clunk her brother in the head with it. Faith enjoyed fun evenings with the kids and sometimes going to bed early when they did, even if that was at six thirty. Sometimes it was exactly what the doctor ordered. Sometimes she'd wonder what it would be like if Frank got home and didn't make her uneasy. Sometimes she'd wonder what it would be like if he never came home at all.

Faith awoke in a panic a few times during the night. Another minute and it would be the next day. The pit in her stomach made her ill. *Who was he with? What was he doing with her?*

A full hour later, a key scratched the metal over and over. The knob jiggled. Once he figured out how to enter the house he stumbled in with a long belch.

"Wonderful." Faith rolled her eyes, getting up to meet him at the door, repulsed by his stench. "You drove like this? You could have killed someone or yourself."

"I'm fine. Leee me alone."

"You're not fine, Frank. This is ridiculous. The fact that you don't see this is a problem ... You're not a kid anymore, you're not in college and this has to stop."

"I only started drinking in college."

"That was almost twenty years ago," she blurted. "You can't go out and party all the time. You have responsibilities now."

He tried to continue to argue his point, but it came out as nonsense.

Faith went to get him a drink of water and thought she heard retching. When she returned he was lying in a pile of his own vomit. Faith ran to him. “Get up. Our new carpet.” She slapped him.

“Don’t worry about it.”

She slapped him harder. “Why do you need to drink to oblivion? When you feel a buzz, just stop, like normal people.”

He groaned and rolled the other way. She scrubbed cleanser on the area, and sprayed his face for good measure. “Wipe your face and get up. I’m so tired of this. When are you going to stop? When are you going to go to AA?”

He groaned.

Faith left him on the floor. She had no idea what time he made his way into bed that morning, but it was a thousand percent apparent that he had no idea that anything had happened when he woke up. And because Faith cleaned up the evidence, it couldn’t be proven.

“Get up. The Birth-To-Three therapist is coming to the house.”

“Why?”

“Seriously?” Faith rolled her eyes. If she had a dollar for every time he asked questions he knew the answers to. “Cut it out. You know Kyle isn’t “tracking”. Why do I have to keep explaining things to you?”

“I don’t even know what that means.”

“If you stuck around and paid attention, you’d see for yourself. But you don’t. It’s all me. All the time.”

A plump Birth-to-Three therapist stepped up into the living room with a bag full of gear. She was out of breath from the short walk from the driveway even though she couldn't have been more than forty-five years old. Faith put the baby carrier over the wet carpet spot so it would force them to move to a different location. Kyle had therapy services because he "wasn't doing much", even though, he was just a baby, Faith thought, he wasn't *supposed* to be doing much. But he wasn't achieving his basic milestones, and that was enough for concern. Faith didn't notice. In her eyes, Kyle was perfect. She watched while the therapist reached into her endless bag and displayed all kinds of exciting visuals. She revealed squeaky toys, toys that sounded like drums, animals whose eyes popped out on springs, colorful stuffies, black and white squiggly pictures, zigzags, shapes, and patterns for Kyle to enjoy. Her pen kept scribbling notes, more frantic with each observation. She oscillated the objects from the left, back to the right, and eventually shook them square in front of his face. Nothing. No response. Faith held in a gasp every time. Thirty minutes of times to be exact. "OK, I'll be back next week to do this again?" She shut her notebook and slammed her hand on top.

"Great," Faith motioned a thumbs-up and a fake smile. Her cheeks reddened, feeling like she was replicating the choreography from her second grade square dance. The truth was that she also had no idea what it all meant. "Have a good weekend!" Faith leaned up against the door swallowing the tears back. *He'll catch up. I know he will.*

Frank brushed by. He had conveniently missed the appointment.

"We need to talk."

"About what?"

"About your drinking."

"It's not that bad."

"You have a problem."

Frank looked past her.

"Do you remember passing out last night?"

Frank remained silent.

"See, you have no idea. You're choosing alcohol over your family, Frank."

"Yeah, okay. You're choosing the kids over me."

Faith squinted at him. Thoughts ricocheted inside her head on how to help him, but what came out was nagging. Maybe he needed chores to keep him busy so he wouldn't drink, but Frank perceived that as telling him what to do. Maybe he needed more space, but that gave him a free pass to leave the house. Maybe she needed to initiate sex or at least pretend to be interested, but the kids were so needy and Kyle was constant. Faith didn't know how to make the whole situation better. She needed to figure out how to make Frank happy and then it would all be better. Simple.

Faith waited for Frank to pull in the driveway from work. She told him that she had something special planned and that he needed to be home. When he came in the house, she surprised him at the stairs wearing brand new lingerie.

"High and tight." Frank blurted. He hated when she wore her hair up and could see nothing else. She chose to ignore him, directing him to the stairs, unbuttoning his shirt. At the second button, she pressed her lips against his. "My friend Dianna took the kids for a little while."

He pushed her away. "I'm hungry."

"We can eat later." She pulled him toward the bedroom where candles reflected and relaxing music played softly.

He looked around and snickered. "This ain't Days of Our Lives". She stood in front of him. Vulnerable. He didn't kiss her back or touch her. He hardly even looked at her.

Faith threw her hands up. "Look, I'm trying here. That's more than I can say for you. You know what, forget it." She blew the candles out, threw clothes on and went downstairs to make dinner. "Idiot. Why do I bother? Do I want to be in this or what? He's not even trying." She paced. Ten minutes later, Faith called to him from the kitchen. "I thought you were hungry." Frank sounded … busy so Faith went up to see what he was doing. Frank tried minimizing the screen while covering his exposed part with his shirt. "What are you doing? Don't say 'nothing'. You'd rather rub one out watching skanks on the Internet than come looking for me? The kids will be here soon. You know what? This is over. I'm done. Who's choosing what now?"

Several minutes later, he joined her in the kitchen without remorse where she was eating alone. She had made chicken over creamy pasta, with fresh buttery garlic spinach. "What the hell is this?" He spat the spinach back on to the plate like a child and jumped up scraping the dinner into the garbage, missing the bag and making a mess. "It tastes like green turd."

Faith tried to stop him. "No. Don't throw the chicken away too." Her voice trailed while she watched him slide the meal into the garbage. "Three year olds do what you just did." Faith's neck started turning the color of radishes, until it reached her cheeks. "I'd *never* do that to you … you know what? I can't Frank … I can't do this anymore." She threw her hands up. "I want a divorce."

"Yeah okay," he mocked and left the house for what she assumed was a liquid dinner.

Faith tried to compose herself before the kids came back. Kyle's Baptism would be in a matter of hours, the next morning in fact, so she couldn't have swollen eyes for the service. Her emotions would have to wait. *Put it in a box*. Put it away like she always did. But Dianna could tell right away.

-4-

They pulled into the church parking lot and before getting out Frank leaned over and whispered; "Don't tell *anyone* about your little plan to destroy our marriage."

Faith nearly strangled herself trying to get out of the car. "All you have to do is get help."

"It's not as bad as you think."

"That's the problem. You don't know how bad it is," her voice got louder.

"Shhh," Frank hissed.

"Don't you dare. I'm *telling* you how bad it is." She waited until his eyes met hers. "You have a problem. And if you don't get help, you're going to lose us." She pulled Kyle's carrier out. He was dressed in a crisp white christening outfit complete with a tiny white vest and baby tie.

"Frank, oh Frank, it's so good to see you." One of his middle-aged Aunties barreled over; the rolls on her arms rippled as she waved. "What a perfect family you have."

Dad of the year. Faith thought, remembering to smile and nod politely.

"Faith, yowsah, come over here! Girl, you are such a blessin' to our family. I swear, the holy heavens opened up and sent you to us when you showed up. You're wicked good for him."

Frank smirked in Faith's direction.

"He makes it difficult sometimes." Faith shot him a look instructing him to behave. But with Auntie's stamp of approval, he could do no wrong.

"Speaking of the heavens, I heard you're singing a special song and…" she clutched her chest, "you have the voice of an angel."

Faith thanked her. "Yes, I'm memorized and ready to go. Although I haven't opened my mouth to sing in public since Jenna's baptism." Faith recalled the night she quit singing because every time she left the house to practice or perform it was an excuse for Frank to drink into oblivion. It was just easier for her to stay home. In the beginning, he stayed home too.

"Aw," Auntie Kelly interrupted her thoughts. "I was hoping it would be true. I can't wait. Now, let me have that precious baby." She whisked him away with Jenna tagging along, happy as could be. "I can't believe he's so little," her voice trailed.

And there it was, an unintentional dig. Yes, he was little. Yes, he was sickly. Yes, he was a few months old already and looked like a newborn. So what. He would get there, Faith vowed.

It wasn't even minutes before Kyle's screech pierced the air and childless Auntie didn't know what to do; handing the carrier to Faith almost as quickly as she stole him away.

"Give him to Frank."

"He wants you," Frank said and ran in the other direction like a child.

The Baptism and reception at the adjoining church hall

went on. Faith and Frank sat together. The rest of the family had no clue that trouble was brewing. Frank reached for the second bottle of beer when the clock struck eleven thirty.

Faith put her hand out. "You've had enough," she reprimanded.

"Oh let him have another, he deserves it. Hard workin' man and all." Faith cringed with growing hatred toward his family's ignorance. "Feed him bread like his grandmother used to do when grandpa had too much to drink. We need some soppage over here." She giggled.

"At least it's over and he can't drink too much more." Dianna said. Dianna, her best friend since grammar school, was the only one who knew. They'd been through so much together; puberty, first boyfriends, breakups, Dianna's first marriage and the trauma that she'd endured there. In fact, Dianna was instrumental in helping Faith choose life for Kyle when the doctors instructed her it would be better to abort him.

"Something's wrong," the doctors had insisted, but no one knew what, even after running blood tests and the amniocentesis.

"It's all your decision," was the only thing that Frank could say. Faith knew that choosing life for Kyle would ultimately be her decision, but she thought that Frank would be there to help and support her. Soon he began proving what he meant. It would be up to Faith all the time.

"Thanks for coming Dianna!"

"Little Mister's Baptism? I wouldn't miss it. How are you … doing?" She almost didn't complete her thought.

"I'm good." Faith nodded, then shook her head. "It's

hard."

"That's because you have an asshole husband who doesn't help you." She looked for the pastor who was at the other end of the room, shaking hands and nodding to family members. "Oops!" They laughed. "But that's changing tonight. Come to the movies with me tonight."

"Oh…" Faith hesitated, looking at Frank and an inconsolable Kyle. Aunties and friends were passing him around to soothe him; bouncing, kissing, making faces. "I can't …" She saw Kyle being handed to her in slow motion while Frank turned away. "You know what? Yes, I'll go. That would be amazing!" Kyle stopped fussing as soon as he heard Faith's voice and she held the pacifier in place in his mouth with her index finger.

"Great! I'll come get you at six forty-five."

Frank managed to keep it together for the brunch reception and they were home by mid-afternoon. All public crises averted, due to Faith's careful planning of an early service. And the soppage.

Both kids were sufficiently tuckered out. Kyle from crying his head off and Jenna from running around like a princess in her white heart tights and patent leather shoes, getting all the attention she wanted from the aunties and older cousins. "I'm going to go to that movie I've been wanting to see with Dianna tonight."

"What movie?"

"The movie. The one I told you about that I wanted to see. We tried to see a couple times before but something always came up."

"Well, tonight's not good."

"What is your problem?"

"Nothing. I mean, you get to go out and I have to stay

here to babysit the kids?"

"When's the last time *I've* been out? You have big plans later? Getting drunk? Meeting someone?"

"What?" He fidgeted. "No," he whined like a child caught in a lie. "But I was planning on going out."

"Always. Look, you already had your drinks today. You don't need more. And it's not called *babysitting* by the way. They're *your* kids too."

"You're the mom."

"What does that mean?"

"You know how to take care of them. I don't."

"Well, it's time you learn. The movie is two hours. You can handle it. Besides, they'll be in bed most of the time once you get them down. Jenna can help you with Kyle. She knows how."

"No."

"What do you mean, 'No'?"

"No." He stomped up the stairs like a spoiled child.

Faith reached for the phone. "Dianna." Faith blurted out when Dianna's voicemail beeped. "I can't go tonight. You're right. I married an inconsiderate asshole and I can't go." Faith trudged up the stairs and sat on her bed, pulling on a pair of crumpled sweat pants and throwing her hair into a messy bun. "Why? Why is this okay?" She whispered, shaking her head. She clasped her hands over her mouth rocking back and forth for several minutes looking around the room. She caught a glimpse of her younger, happy self in a frame on the dresser. Frank was tipsy, kissing her on the cheek. Her smile lit up the room. "You stupid, stupid girl." She grabbed the photo. "Don't you see the clues? He's showing you loud and clear." She smashed the frame on the dresser, the glass shattered.

Jenna heard the noise. "Mama?"

"I'll be right down honey." Faith shoved the frame in her drawer. "Well, there's my answer. He doesn't care about me, he didn't even yell up to find out what happened. He'll never change. But I'm stuck. I can't divorce him. Kyle and Frank *cannot* be Jenna's responsibility when I'm not around. I cannot do that to her. I need to do what's best for my children."

At six forty-five Dianna showed up. "Are you ready?"

"You didn't get my message? I can't go."

"Look. You're going. You never do anything for yourself. Get in the car. We're going." She said loud enough for Frank to hear. He was slouched in his recliner watching sports as usual.

"Let me get the kids ready first."

"Frank can do it. Right, Frank?"

Frank didn't want to blow his cover so Mister Charming pretended to be capable. The truth was that Faith knew the kids were pretty much all set for bed anyway, and not much needed to be done. "OK, kiss Mommy."

"Kai [Can I] come?"

"Next time! You're going to spend Daddy-and-Me time. I love you."

"I la uooo too Mama!"

Frank huffed.

Faith and Dianna rolled their eyes. "I don't have my purse." Faith said.

"You mean your *diaper bag*?" Dianna teased. "I got you, don't worry. This one's on me." Dianna shoved Faith out the door.

Faith picked at her cuticle, nervous to leave Frank with the kids, but happy to be out. After smothering their popcorn with extra butter and salt, they chatted like little girls until the beginning credits started and laughed and cried throughout the entire movie whether it was sad or not. When it was over, they and most of the women in the audience remained frozen in their seats, mesmerized from watching the hot guy of the year shake his man parts on the big screen in front of them. Some women were fanning themselves, some were laughing.

Faith tried to get up, but fell back in the chair, making her giggle. “I can't get up.”

“Yeah girl, you couldn't keep your eyes off of him! You should have seen yourself when he took his pants off and started dancing.”

“You, me and every other woman in this audience.”

A twosome behind them laughed and agreed.

“OK let's go.” Dianna said, standing over her.

“Seriously, I can't move. I need a minute.” Faith hunched over. “I'm gonna pee my pants.”

Dianna laughed.

“Oh no.” Faith hunched over.

“Are you ok?” Dianna tried to not make Faith laugh and make it worse. She knew that once she started, it wouldn’t end well.

“Nope. I need my adult diaper and my walker.” The laughter began. “Stop making me laugh.”

“You know this isn’t me Miss Laugh 'Til I Pee My Pants.” Dianna directed Faith to the restroom. She waited outside the door but Faith didn’t come out.

Faith dabbed her eyes, but didn’t know if her tears were from laughing or crying or a combination of both.

She pressed her fingers deep into her eye sockets, but the tears still poured out. Her body shook, trying to prevent a full-fledged sob session. Dianna stood outside the stall and tried to calm her.

Faith whimpered. "I can't stop."

"It's okay, I'm here. Can you come out?"

After several more minutes, Faith released the latch and the door creaked open. "I'm sorry for ruining the night." She splashed water on her face.

Dianna handed her a paper towel and linked her arm with Faith's. Their matching butterfly tattoos showed when their wrists pressed together. "Don't worry about me. I'm worried about you."

"I'll be fine. I mean, he needs to go to AA, but he doesn't think he has a problem."

"What about Al-Anon? For yourself?"

"I've looked into that actually. But he has to fix the problem in order for it to get better for all of us."

"Well, that could be a start for you at least, talk to people who've been through it." She started the car when Faith blurted out. "I told him I want a divorce."

Dianna put the car back in park to look Faith's way. "I figured it was something like that."

"You knew?"

"You're the only one who didn't."

Faith's eyes widened.

"But you know what," Dianna continued. "It wouldn't be the worst thing. Your stress level is sky-high and maybe it will force him to have some responsibility."

"Yeah right."

"Well, if he doesn't, he won't see the kids. Simple as that."

Simple as that. It had been almost twelve minutes since they pulled into her driveway. She could see Frank pacing and looking out the window. Her stomach tightened. She saw the light from the television flashing in the living room and knew that the kids were asleep. Frank began striking the curtains open and shut. A pain gripped Faith's abdomen. Another minute went by.

"I don't know why he can't stop drinking. And when he tries to … he's still a jerk. He wasn't like this when we first met."

"Well, that's not exactly true." Dianna put the car in park.

"You're saying you knew he was a jerk?"

"I'm saying he had us all fooled, me included, and I see them all coming a mile away since … my ex."

"You're wrong."

"I'm never wrong and you know it."

"You didn't say anything."

"Give me a break. You were so blinded when he started talking to you that night at the bar," Dianna said. "And with each drink, he got more and more … charming."

Faith grunted at the memory. "We had to drive him home. He said he never did that before and that he was embarrassed."

"Warning." Dianna cleared her throat. "We should have paid more attention."

Faith raised her eyebrows. "Well, you didn't exactly tell me that night."

"You're kidding me, right? You wouldn't have listened. You were fresh off a break up from the love-of-your-life-the-bachelor-doctor who broke your heart and stomped all over it with a "break-up freedom party" that you weren't invited to."

"How'd you remember that?"

"Oh, I remember everything. And — Dean was there that night too."

"Dean? I haven't thought of him in years."

"Yup, he was there too. The perfect storm!" Dianna's mischievous grin widened. "Dean, the boy you were head over heels in love with in high school, but never talked to. The adorable blond hockey player you hooked up with years later in college, but you were a naïve virgin who didn't know anything about anything, including grooming your lady parts and that scared him away I'm sure and he moved on to the next flavor and broke your heart too."

"Wow. Harsh. Thanks for the reminder."

"The point was Dean was there. Remember? And because you were mad at him, and the doctor, and this douche-bag Frank…" she pointed to the curtains flapping in the window, "was paying you all kinds of attention, you told Dean that he had his chance and you proceeded to shove it in his face. And then we had to bring your new idiot home."

Faith looked at her surprised. "Yeah. All that happened, didn't it?"

"Well look at how that turned out." Frank was still snatching the curtains back and forth like it was some sort of Morse code. "En-neey-way… my point is …" Dianna continued, "you need to put your big girl pants on and he needs to go to AA to fix this. Now."

Dianna was right. Faith couldn't go on like this. They couldn't stay married like this. Faith had a medically complex child who needed her attention; she couldn't worry about an incapable husband too. Dianna had experience with both so Faith knew to listen and that Dianna would be there for her no matter what.

Dianna was one of the first in the group to live the fairytale, get married and have a wonderful baby to make their lives complete and blissfully happy. But it was a lie. Marriage was a lot of work, and having a child with special needs put extra stress on an otherwise hard marriage, friendships too. No one knew what to say when Dianna's daughter Alicia was born "different", but everyone had hope that she would survive. She just had to get strong enough.

When Alicia beat the odds the first few months and was allowed to go home with breathing and feeding tubes and a whole list of instructions and precautions, Faith was there to help. When Dianna was deserted but showed ultimate strength and independence, doing everything on her own, Faith took note. Surely Faith would choose a husband who would be more supportive and her children would be perfectly healthy, she thought. It was an odd and rare hand dealt to her friend, but it wouldn't happen to her.

As the months went on and Alicia became stronger, they believed, small progresses were huge wins in their minds, even against doctor's grim predictions. She would talk and walk one day. Whether it was through lots of therapies, or through sheer prayer and determination, she would walk, God Damn It, she would walk. But she never did.

Alicia's favorite stuffed comfy was a yellow butterfly ballerina. She wore ballet shoes on her feet and a crooked pink tutu. It made her smile and laugh every time she saw it presented in front of her face. She roared with joy when she saw it. Her arms flapped, but she couldn't reach out to grasp it. It became her symbol of strength and all the she'd overcome. *Change. Fly. Soar.*

A few years went by and she was wheelchair bound and needed a ventilator to breathe. And even though kids stared at the playground and Alicia couldn't participate, Dianna still brought her there each week. She loved to see the other children play and she laughed and grunted whenever they ran by. Faith was there with Dianna through it all. She was there when Alicia took her last breath; a moment a parent should never have to endure. Expected, but not. She was there when Dianna wailed in agony and didn't want to leave her only child at the cemetery under the pile of yellow and pink carnations, until they had to escort her away.

Faith recalled their conversation when they knew something would be wrong with Kyle, but they didn't know what. Doctors wanted her to abort him. He might have Downs. He might have Trisomy 18. He might have this or that or something or nothing, but no one knew what. Faith didn't know what to do. But she saw Dianna's strength and that was enough to make her choose life for him. Frank had already made it clear that she'd be on her own if she chose him. The statistics were not definitive enough for her to make a choice in the other direction.

"Faith, the life of a special needs child is hard. So hard." She reached for Faith's hand. Faith vividly remembered the conversation. "But only you can make that decision for you."

"I don't have it in me Dianna. I don't think I have it in me to take care of a special needs child. I don't know if I can do it."

"I didn't think I could either –." She looked toward the floor. "It was unimaginable. It's still unimaginable and the most painful experience of my life. But you won't have the same thing, it may not be as bad."

"You don't know that."

"I know, I don't. I'm trying to be positive here. But you were there for me. And no matter what, I'll be there for you too. And for the record, I wouldn't have changed a thing."

When Kyle was born, Dianna scooped him up and held her promise from day one.

They were interrupted by the floodlight flicking on and off from the driveway. "You better go inside before Frank busts a gasket."

"Do I have to?" Faith sighed.

"Do you want me to go in with you? Kick his ass?"

"No, I think he's doing that all on his own." They chuckled, watching the curtains chop back and forth like he was sending smoke signals for them to stop having a great 'ole time in the driveway.

"Where the hell were you?"

"You know we were at the movies."

"Three hours ago. Why were you sitting in the car for so long? Why are you crying? Did you tell her?" Frank peppered her with questions.

"Frank," Faith put her hand up to stop him. She sighed. "Dianna's my friend. Things here aren't exactly going like I planned. I'm not happy and I need to talk it out."

"You weren't supposed to tell anyone."

"Why? So you can keep hiding? This isn't working. You need to go to AA and get help for yourself."

"Just because you *think* I have a problem doesn't mean I do." He stood in front of her shaking like a druggie waiting for his next hit.

"Why are you shaking?"

"Don't worry about it." He grabbed his jacket and keys.

"Sure. That's always your answer. Run. Go. You need help. You need AA. You need a sponsor."

He whisked by her.

"I'll help you." Her words followed him out the door.

-5-

Faith didn't know where Frank slept that night. She turned the news on to make sure there were no drunken deaths in town overnight; a terrible way to wake up from a night of no sleep, but better than a knock on the door from the police, she supposed. Whenever Kyle woke to drink a few ounces, Faith checked the bed, the floor and the bathroom, no sign of Frank.

The sky lightened a bit and she knew that it had to have been around six AM when she heard a noise. The kids would be up soon. She couldn't let them see whatever condition he was in. She intercepted him at the door.

"This cannot keep happening."

Faith held her breath as he pushed past her, looking like hell. He barely made it to the bathroom with his knees on the tile when Jenna appeared in the doorway to witness his head in the toilet.

"Dada sick."

"Something like that."

"I make better."

"Get her out of here," he croaked.

"No Daddy," Jenna's eyes widened, "I make better."

"Go," he barked.

Jenna's lip quivered.

"Jenna, come help Mama. Daddy will be fine. He needs some privacy." Faith whispered to Frank on the way out. "You're ruining this family and since you're doing nothing to help yourself, I want out." Jenna followed Faith put on a recording of one of her favorite shows; the one with the singing men in their brightly colored shirts and silly red car. She glued herself to the screen instantly. Faith sat beside her.

"Snack Mama?" Faith obliged, trying not to hear Frank's heaves.

When Faith went in to check on him, mostly to see if he was still breathing, he was resting his face on the rim.

"What the hell? Gross."

"He looked up; face full of tears. "I don't know what's wrong with me."

Faith took a step back. She bit her lip and her tone softened. "*I do* ... You have a problem."

"I don't know why I do this."

"You need help." She rubbed the top of his back between his shoulder blades. "You cannot do it on your own any longer. You need to go to AA. You need to get a sponsor."

"But I'm not an alcoholic."

Faith sighed and stood up. "That's the problem, Frank. You are. The first step is admitting it."

"Yeah okay." His words hit her with such rude indifference toward her, toward her family, that it made her want to push his head in the toilet.

"Look," Faith stopped. "You have no other options. Choose alcohol or choose us. It's up to you."

The tears streamed down his face again. "I want to be a good father. I want to be a good husband. But I don't know how."

"The first step is AA. I'll go with you." She touched his arm.

"You'll do that for me?"

"Will you go otherwise?"

Frank remained silent.

They sat stalling in the church hall parking lot that night in the adjacent town, until a stranger startled them with a tap on the window. They must have been used to newbies losing courage. Frank had no way of backing out. "Come in," he said. He smelled like an ashtray. "You can sit with me."

After grabbing coffee and snacks, everyone took turns announcing their names and when it was Frank's turn, Faith was surprised to hear him parrot the words. "Hi, I'm Frank and I'm an alcoholic." The words came out. Perhaps even Frank didn't believe it after he said it.

"I'm so proud of you," Faith leaned over, reaching for Frank's hand. "You can do this," Faith said. He interlocked his fingers in hers and kissed her on the cheek. At the end, he was inundated with pamphlets and the business cards of people to call, day or night, they would help him if he had the urge to pick up a drink, they'd be there for him. If he called.

That night, Faith believed he was truly going to stay sober, forever. He needed to hit rock bottom, she thought, and since it had happened, he would finally be able to stay sober for good. He didn't want his children to see him lying on the bathroom floor. He didn't want to be divorced. He made the first step by going to AA and that proved that he was serious. He wanted to change.

Faith felt a closeness to him that had been missing for a long time. Frank stayed home that night and they had dinner together as a family. No phones, no television interrupted them. He helped feed the kids without incident. He read stories to them, and helped with the bedtime routine. Jenna cuddled into the crook of his arm and Faith smiled. This was the father that Faith had always wanted for them, the perfect little family she had always hoped was possible. He was doing it, and her heart burst with love. She knew he could do it. He was home and not distracted. He was sober. *Sober!* It didn't matter if it seemed like a week, a day, or even hours. This was a big step and he needed to know that she appreciated it. In a quiet house, the children asleep, with no game on, they fell into a rhythm that used to be so natural for them. Before falling asleep on his chest she whispered, "I'm so glad you're sober. I missed you. I missed us." She wiped a single tear from her cheek she didn't let him see.

Stepping into her parents' house was like being transported into a time warp. Floral drapes framed lacy sheer panels, with matching valances and tiebacks. The oversized chintz couch matched the window treatments. Wall-to-wall carpeting spanned every inch of the house, even up the stairs. Gaudy perfection masked the tears she'd shed as a child. Returning to the house brought back all the emotions as if she still lived there.

Her mother had asked all the typical questions about how everyone had been, but she never actually listened to the answers.

"Yeah, yeah, yeah," was her response before Faith even had a chance to answer. She wasn't sure why it bothered her so much; her mother had always been that way. Faith stopped mid-sentence and her mother didn't even notice. She bit her lip to cover the sting. *She'll never change*. Her headshake turned into a nod, masking the hurt of the past. Why dwell? Faith had come out on the other side. A successful workingwoman in the corporate world, even when Jenna was born, she worked. She had a house and a family. Faith had put her past behind her. Her mother's sharp tongue, the insults, the neglect. She'd forgiven and forgotten. She thought. But returning back to the house always stirred up things she hadn't expected.

There was a point when she had wanted her mother's approval more than life itself. But she didn't need that now. She was an adult, in reality, if not in her mother's eyes. She had her own family; a husband who was sober now and who could listen. Children with whom she could be best friends with and share stories and real emotions. Children that she always held and cuddled and vowed to never beat or degrade like her mother had. Children she loved with all of her heart. Her mind was decades away with painful memories when her mother's voice startled her.

"Grandpa." The shrill tone of her voice reverberated through the house. She'd called him "Grandpa" the millisecond the grandchildren were born, maybe even in utero. "Grandpa, get the camera," her mother ordered.

"Yes Babs." His head hung like a scolded dog. He went, opening and closing the honey oak veneer cabinet doors in the kitchen, not knowing where to look.

After thirty-seconds of the Faith and Babs stare-down, her mother huffed and stomped out of the room to show him where it was in plain view in the back of a cabinet. A cabinet full of hoarder's essentials that had been stuffed away, her own late mother's salt and peppershakers, and various lead crystal pieces and junk favorites. It was this junk that Faith had longed to own; a piece of her favorite grandmother; the grandmother who taught her unconditional maternal love, the junk her mother would commit to the darkness, never to see the light of day, never to be loved and remembered; punished.

Bab's grandchildren were her outward pride and joy.

She would gush about them to anyone nearby, but helping Faith watch them or to give her a break was like asking her to do taxes. She'd offered that Faith could bring them over any time, but only when it was convenient. In times when Faith was desperate for a break, she would think about dropping the kids off with her, even so she could nap for an hour. With her father around, her mother would be nice to them, she knew. She'd proven herself so far, showering the grandkids with extra love to make up for her past bad behavior. Faith was shocked that her mother had possessed any maternal instincts and was a little jealous that none of it was directed toward her. Maybe a convenient time would come when her mother could help out more. But perhaps since Frank was finally sober, he could take more responsibility and her break would actually happen. Better late than never, she thought.

Jenna pulled out the basket of toys and coloring books from the corner that Babs had instructed was especially for her. Kyle was being extra adorable at the moment. Doing what? Faith didn't know. What did infants do? Nothing much. Being cute at sleeping of course. But Babs had to capture it on film for subsequent boasting at work parties and such. Faith understood though. When Jenna was born, she watched her in awe for hours while she slept, inspecting her perfect hands, feet, face, simply watching her breathe. With Kyle, his sleeping sessions were few and far between. He'd be stirring soon enough so she hoped he'd stay asleep a little longer.

Frank was alert, attentive, even making silly jokes. Faith's heart skipped at the vision of the perfect family that she'd always longed for.

"I'm so proud of you," Faith whispered to him.

Frank grabbed Faith and pulled her toward him in one swoop, pressing his lips on hers while Jenna was turned away. Faith giggled from being startled, but squirmed with excitement by the sentiment.

"You two seem … cozy." Her father interrupted.

Heat flooded Faith's cheeks. "Sorry Dad." Faith and Frank giggled like teenagers being caught, about to be reprimanded. But the truth was that it was the first time they'd smiled together in a while. She enjoyed feeling close to him emotionally, physically.

"I want a family photo," Babs blurted out, unable to figure out how to remove the cover on the lens.

"Grandpa, come here," she demanded. "I can't figure out this camera. I want a picture." Faith's father obliged rolling his eyes. That family photo, the best they would ever take, solidified Thanksgiving and the definition of hope; hope of better things to come. Hope of a tumultuous past staying far in the past. Hope of never having to endure it again. Hope of a new beginning of love, trust, and peace; the new definition of forever. The kids were plopped into their laps and Faith put her hand on Frank's arm, feeling security and contentment. She breathed a sigh of relief that was captured in the family photo for perpetuity. She couldn't have been happier until Frank interrupted her.

"I've been doing so good. I can have one beer." He told her father.

Faith's heart sank. "No ... you can't have just one." She tried to keep her voice at a whisper. Her blood pressure rose and she felt her stomach knot up.

"I'm kidding," he said. "I figured, since it's a holiday. But I understand. I'll stick with soda."

Relief washed over her. "Don't scare me like that." He wouldn't fall back into his old ways. He couldn't. She let him cuddle her and she welcomed the closeness. "Maybe we can put the kids to bed early." It wasn't a question as much as it had been a statement. Frank's new found sobriety was a turn-on and she wasn't going to let the moment go unpraised.

"Can we leave now," Frank whispered.

"Hey, no secrets you too," Jenna pouted.

Faith's face reddened.

Jenna and Kyle's bedtime routines went as planned, they were sufficiently tired out from the grandparent's house. When Faith met Frank in the bedroom, he took the time to see her, to really see her. It was different than Frank's usual non-foreplay which meant that he whipped out his man part in her face expecting her immediate arousal. But this time, she felt close to him, in love. He took an extra few minutes to undress her, to touch her and pull her close. Her body responded. But the rhythm sped up and she knew it would be over soon, so she hurried to get there with him, falling onto his chest when it was over. Pleased with herself for making it happen.

She fell asleep with her mind racing. She hated thinking mode. She wished he would spend more time pleasing her, but it had happened at least. She hated that her mind drifted off to being nervous for the other shoe to drop because it always did. *I can't believe he thought he could have one beer. But he didn't. He's sober. It's going to work this time. He realizes everything he has to lose. He's back.*

We're back. And this can only get better.

-7-

Faith fell into a dreamy sense of hope over the next several weeks. Frank went to work every day and was home every night, except for AA meetings or nights he needed to call his sponsor. He watched his sports at home with a soda instead of hanging out alone at the bar.

It was unseasonably warm for New England. Faith ran to open windows and let the fresh air in. The neighborhood kids buzzed by wearing sweatshirts and shorts with their caps hanging backward; cards fluttered in the spokes as they rode by and she chuckled that the fad had come back around. She caught a whiff of the apple tree outside the window, which always reminded her of her precious grandmother's house. She had to have an apple tree on her property when she grew up and when this house had one; she knew it was a sign that her grandmother was looking over her.

"Let's go out for a walk, as a family. The craft fair is happening at the green." Faith announced when Frank walked by to see what she was looking at. Jenna bounced around like she'd been given candy for breakfast. Faith got the stroller ready and parked it in front of the house. Her family was whole again.

While they walked, Jenna hung on to Frank. She didn't want to be pushed on the sit-and-stand stroller behind Kyle and didn't want to walk, so Frank carried her until she got too heavy. Faith tried to coax her into the stroller while Jenna whined louder.

"You're causing a scene." Frank warned Faith.

"Me?" Faith opened her mouth, stunned. Everyone knows that children have a fit sometimes." She kept walking and left Kyle with Jenna and Frank.

"Mama," Jenna ran to Faith. Frank grumbled obscenities and started to push the stroller to meet them. A family was coming up the sidewalk toward them and Jenna's eyes lit up at the balloons and lollipops in the other children's' hands. Frank sped up passing Faith, gaining on the other family. "Let them pass," Faith ordered. Frank didn't listen, forcing the other family off the sidewalk into the grass. Faith apologized to them as she passed, hanging her head.

"It's okay," the woman said.

"That's not the point." They continued on without stopping.

"What the hell?" Faith whispered, trying not to let Jenna hear.

But Jenna must have sensed the tension and ran to Frank. "Pick me up." She demanded. Frank left the stroller, whisked her in his arms and carried her a quarter mile toward the green in a huff. Faith slowed down to let them go ahead. When they were out of sight, she turned around and pushed the stroller back home, leaving Frank to deal with Jenna alone. When she returned home, she knew she had a few minutes to cool off before they returned. Her perfect family dreams, crushed again. "What is wrong with him? He's sober. So why is he acting like a jerk?" She looked out the window. "Why do I keep expecting things to change?"

The ringer was off on Faith's phone but she saw it lighting up. Frank. She didn't answer. She washed her face with cold water and tried to gain her composure before he came home. She practiced one of her favorite moments, sitting on the floor with Kyle in her lap. She had time to gather all the necessary things: the tarp, the bottle, blankets, and snacks for Jenna. She knew Jenna would find comfort in helping with Kyle's feeding when she returned. Jenna ran straight to them and cuddled up next to them, resting her feet on Faith's lap. Frank entered, yelling. "Where were you?" He stood over them.

"I had to come back," Faith said. "You want to talk about what happened with the family on the sidewalk?"

His arms began to swing around.

"Back up." Faith warned.

Jenna started tapping her feet on Faith's lap, then giving love taps on Kyle's shoulder, then rested her little feet on his head. The taps continued. "No, we have to be careful," Faith reminded her. But in typical toddler fashion, Jenna started to kick harder and faster, telltale remnants from a missed nap.

"I can't believe you're letting her kick him in the head," Frank yelled.

"I'm not." Faith tried to get up, but toppled over; Kyle in her arms. She started to giggle. She tried to move Kyle away, but Frank was in the way in front of her and Jenna's feet were swinging on her side. She couldn't get up on her knees quick enough. She fumbled around, one hand with the baby, one hand with the bottle. Frank grabbed Jenna and put her in her room. When he returned, Faith was still trying to stand up. Nervous laughter started up again as he approached. "What just happened?" She asked.

"What do you mean? You let her kick him in the head and now you're laughing? Now I've seen it all." He repeated and paced back and forth, looking up and raising his arms as if he was performing a miracle in church complete with halleluiahs.

The more she tried to stop laughing, the angrier he became. He hadn't taken the time to know her enough to understand this quirk about her; laughing fits as a child in church while her mother pinched her under the songbook to shut up, her defense mechanisms in full-force. She doubled over, counting the seconds for him to leave because, after all, he always did. *Why was he having a fit? What happened on the way to the green? Why does he think this is okay?* Faith didn't understand. He stood over her hyperventilating body on the floor, mocking her.

The sunlight disappeared when he shut the front door. He was free to go, again, and she was stuck. Stuck at home. Stuck in the marriage. Stuck as the sole caregiver, of everyone including him, with no reprieve. Stuck with an addict, but he was sober. Maybe it would be better if he had one drink to take the edge off, but she knew he couldn't stop there. Anger bubbled up inside her and she rose to her knees. She let out a deep wail. A cry for lost hope, for happiness that fell into the ditch when that family fell off the sidewalk. As loud as she could, her voice raspy and raw, she screamed, "You're making me hate you." Her voice echoed. The door flung open. Her eyes widened and she inhaled, trying to back up but he stood over her.

“What did you say?” Frank confronted her.

She pulled Kyle closer to her breast and stood up to Frank. “You’re making me hate you,” she repeated, quieter but cold. She didn’t take her eyes off of him.

“Yeah okay, it’s *my* fault.” Frank said.

“I thought you quit drinking.”

“I did.”

“Well, something’s wrong. You need to go get checked out. Maybe you need anxiety meds.”

“I’m fine.”

“Obviously you’re not.” She focused her eyes on him.

A silent battle ensued of who would make the next move. Frank backed away from her, slamming the front door on his way out. His car skid out of the driveway, again. Horns beeped. He beeped back. Expletives echoed down the street. She exhaled, realizing she’d been holding her breath the whole time. Until Jenna peeked around the corner.

Faith kept busy during the days with what should have been bonding time with the new baby and family … maternity leave from work was nearly ending and she’d have to go back to work full-time. But how? Her days were jam-packed with appointments either at doctor’s offices, hospitals, or in the house. Every time, there was a new symptom to check which meant that new services were added from Birth-to-Three including physical therapy, which Kyle absolutely hated. Faith held her breath at each visit waiting for a new devastating health problem to check. New specialists kept being added to the growing list to figure out what was wrong. How many doctors could there be for a tiny human who'd lived only a few months? There were no answers in sight.

Multiple appointments in one day, several appointments a week, feeding test days, and an apnea test was added. Faith had to do it all alone while Frank was at work. Jenna was dragged along bored out of her skull or worried about her little "brudder", but Faith had no other choice than to bring her. Jenna missed going to daycare, but since Faith was home, Frank deemed daycare costs unnecessary and refused to take time off for appointments.

The night of the sleep apnea test was difficult but Faith couldn't imagine having to endure such an appointment while having to work the next day. Kyle woke up all night long which was expected since he had wires glued all over his little head and body. Had either of them slept at all? Soon, a nurse threw the lights on, practically snatching the wires off of him, leaving the glue which made his hair look spikey. Faith felt like they were being shoved out, like they had overstayed their welcome. She barely had time to get dressed or brush her teeth, instead yawned while dressing Kyle and putting his jacket on. The cool air woke her up when she stepped outside into the darkness. A hint of orange sky confirmed that it was early dawn. Hers was the one lonely car parked in the distance. She picked up speed to get across the desolate parking lot safely and clipped Kyle's carrier into the base. Soon they were on their way to make their hour ride home. Faith rubbed her eyes and focused in front of her before putting the car in gear; she could barely keep her eyes open when her phone rang.

"When are you coming home?" Frank blurted.

She hesitated. "I'm on my way now, what's wrong?"

"Well, hurry up, I have to get to work."

"You know where we are, right? I can only do what I can do. Can you get Jenna ready for the sitter?"

"You're gonna be home, I'm not paying for a sitter."

"Look, I'm exhausted."

"Nap when she naps."

"You know she doesn't nap. What is your problem?" Faith inhaled.

An hour later, her stomach gurgled and a sharp pain nearly doubled her over. She turned down her double-lined road an hour later. Kyle dropped his pacifier, again, and she tried to reach back to put it in his mouth while driving like she always did. She caught a glimpse of Frank's car passing her; driving in the opposite direction. Her head followed him in slow motion and she exhaled, realizing that she had been holding it in for quite some time. She took a deep breath, relieved that she wouldn't have to see him or talk to him. Surely he had brought Jenna to the sitter on his way to work. Faith looked forward to a break while Kyle napped and Jenna would be at the sitter for a few hours at least. When she entered the house, Jenna jumped out from underneath blankets on the couch running toward them. Faith gasped. "Mama, Brudder, I missed you! I la uooo!"

Faith cradled her tightly, holding in her anger. "I la uooo too Miss Jenna. Bunches!" She kissed her all over her soft face.

After Faith got Jenna settled with breakfast and washed the glue out of Kyle's spikey hair, she snuggled up with both of them for a nap. Even though Jenna mostly played and watched TV. Faith would have to deal with Frank another time. There was simply no energy left to spare.

Faith suspected that it hadn't truly been thirty days since Frank became sober because his behaviors resurfaced. He continued to fly into fits of anger and leave to "cool off" somewhere because she left too many spoons in the sink or the clean laundry was still piled "sky-high" in a basket at dinnertime. Why did Faith think that his new-found sobriety, or whatever he was trying to lead himself to believe, would stop his tantrums? Why did Frank think his tantrums were okay, that it was acceptable to leave her alone with all the responsibilities if he was thinking clearly? Faith didn't understand. He wasn't a kid anymore. They had a mortgage. They had children; one, medically complex. She didn't want to do it on her own. She wanted the soccer dad who would kick a ball with them at the park. She wanted to cuddle up with them all and watch movies after supper like he'd told her his father had done with him and his brothers. She wanted that. And sometimes, she thought she could have that with him if he just got help. Faith closed her eyes and prayed that one day Frank would turn himself around. Not for her, but for his kids, for himself. They all deserved that.

A few days earlier Frank was sitting in his recliner,

waving his middle finger at a car that beeped, startling him when they passed the house. "I hate everyone," he spouted.

"What is wrong with you? That's probably someone we know."

Frank couldn't explain.

"Frank, I'm begging you, go to a doctor to help you with whatever is making you anxious. You need medication or something to take the edge off. This isn't working."

Frank told Faith he'd made an appointment but was that only because Faith nagged him? He wouldn't tell her who he saw … or when. She had to trust him. But why? So he didn't have to hold up his end of the bargain of getting help? So he could continue drinking and hope she didn't notice? So she would back off from expecting so much from him? Why did Faith think she didn't deserve an explanation? Why wouldn't Frank talk to her and let her help him? Was the truth harder than the reality? Their marriage was going down the toilet. Fast. And Frank wasn't helping himself to change it. Faith left the room, leaving him sitting in the chair calling after her. She didn't stop.

"Oh my God," Faith inhaled. "He never called to get help." Her eyes opened wide. "He never went to the doctor. And AA? I bet he never went there either…" She slumped down. "This is *never* going to change. I see glimpses that it will be okay, and then just as fast he proves that it won't. He has *no* intention to make this better." She pressed both hands on her chest and exhaled, feeling her heart palpitating. "The good moments … they are so far in the past that I can hardly see them any more.

I can count them on one hand." She nodded. "And the future? Our future?" She chewed the inside of her lip. "I'm always waiting for something bad to happen. And it always does. I cannot keep living like this. I can't remember the last time I was happy. He should want that too."

Getting through a particularly cold autumn cooped up in the house didn't help and Kyle still wasn't doing a whole lot. He didn't respond to a smile. He didn't babble. He didn't reach for toys or hold his own bottle, nothing. Faith didn't know what to make of it. Jenna had made all of her milestones with ease.

The second Faith RSVP'd to Dianna's holiday party, she put the phone down and raced through the house, making lists for what she'd make and bring. Because of Kyle's chronic ear and sinus infections caused by his terrible reflux, they were basically homebound. Faith couldn't wait to feel the closeness of people; a hug, a gesture of encouragement that she was doing a good job. Her mouth watered for weeks thinking about having adult beverages since she couldn't keep alcohol in the pantry for any length of time without it disappearing. No longer would she unwind with a glass of wine after the kids went to bed or add anything fun to a particularly plain drink for fear of Frank relapsing.

The day of the holiday party finally arrived. Faith spent the morning cooking, baking, and gathering all the baby and toddler gear, including pajamas, so she could get Kyle and Jenna changed and into bed right away instead of having to do it when they got home from the party. It had been several hours since Frank left the house that day with no explanation. He'd been acting secretive again and left early in the afternoon with no explanation. Hours later, he hadn't returned. Faith grew angrier with each call that went straight to his voice mail. "He knows we have plans and where." She smashed a dirty mixing spoon into the sink. "Jenna, get your shoes and coat, honey." She called toward the other room. She looked at the clock as she gathered up the sides and baked treats, hoping to leave before Frank showed up. She reached for the doorknob. Too late; he barged in.

"I'm coming with you."

"No, you're not." Faith winced. "You didn't even shower today. You stink."

"You're not going without me." His words were garbled.

"Frank, what happened? You're drunk." She pressed her fingers into her temple waiting for an answer.

He looked down at the floor.

"Why didn't you talk to me? Why didn't you call your sponsor?"

"I only had one."

"Yeah, no. You've been gone all day." She tried to push past him with the bag of dessert.

Frank stood in front of the door. "How will that look if you go without me?"

"How will that look if you show up drunk?"

"I'm not drunk."

"You are, Frank. Get in the shower and sober up."

Faith tried to leave without him while he was in the shower. "Hurry, put your coat on for mama." But Jenna wanted daddy and whined for him. Kyle puked on his outfit. Faith groaned and looked up to the heavens for strength.

As soon as she was done changing Kyle, Frank showed up at the front door, showered but his old clothes were back on; a dirty football sweatshirt with scraggly cuffs, saggy jeans, and worn out sneakers. It was a stark contrast to Faith's festive red sweater, dress pants and boots. Even her hair was brushed and her lips sparkled for the occasion. Her bloodshot eyes refused the added touch of contacts so she kept her glasses on, but besides that, she was ready to go.

Jenna headed straight to Dianna's Christmas tree, her eyes wide when she spotted the presents underneath it. Over the next few hours, Faith was busy trying to have conversations, helping Jenna open presents and taking care of everyone else; cutting up Jenna's food, making Kyle three-ounce bottles in twenty-minute increments. Three ounces was wishful thinking since he only had ever consumed one ounce at a time, inevitably having to throw it away, over and over again, but she was hopeful that one day he'd do it, so she continued to make and throw out half the portion. She hadn't had a chance to eat her own food.

Frank took advantage of being unsupervised until Faith noticed him staggering to the bathroom. Everyone in the house heard him heaving from the middle of the living room. "Is he okay?" They gathered outside the door.

Faith's neck and face turned beet red and Dianna felt

her shame and disappointment. By the time he came out, wiping his mouth with his sleeve, Faith approached him. "We're leaving."

"But we just got here."

"We're leaving."

But leaving with a toddler in feet pajamas, diaper bags, toys, all the gear, and a colicky baby who was hungry all the time, meant that Kyle had to eat first, again. Faith made Frank wait.

"I thought we were leaving."

"I'm making Kyle a bottle."

"What's taking so long?" Frank complained.

Faith fumbled in the kitchen mixing formula, while Dianna tried to help make to-go plates filled with meat, gravy, creamy potatoes, buttery vegetables, whatever would fit on the plates and in containers.

"Do you want dessert?" Dianna asked.

"Um … yeah that will be a necessity. Can you pack the wine for me too?" Faith half-joked. "I'm so sorry," she whispered.

"Been there, remember? I'm here for you. Call me later." Dianna walked her to the door.

"Frank, please carry Jenna. I put her in her jammies already and she can't walk on the cold gravel without shoes."

"Why do I have to do everything?" His arms flailed around.

Faith could see a few people looking on and whispering. She reached down to pick up Kyle's car seat when Dianna's new husband intercepted, pushing his way to the carrier. "I got it, I'd be happy to help. Perhaps my actions will rub off on Dianna here. Babies are so cute, aren't they?" Faith thought they were going to make out right there in the doorway. She rolled her eyes, partly jealous, but mostly happy for her, happy for them.

Faith apologized profusely on the way out but they weren't having any of it. It wasn't Faith's fault. Dianna's husband held Kyle's baby carrier patiently waiting for Frank to settle Jenna in the car seat mid-toddler meltdown. She didn't want her seatbelt strapped for whatever reason. Frank tried to keep her down in order to buckle it. Faith got in the driver's seat to start the car. The overhead light dimmed to pitch black and Frank started yelling, "Why'd you turn the light off?"

No one knew who he was yelling at.

"Jesus." Faith whispered under her breath. "Frank, the light went out because you're taking too long." Faith tilted her head to the back seat where Frank started to screech like a child, biting his tongue. Everyone watched and waited, aghast.

Dianna raised one eyebrow. "Are you sure you'll be okay?" She asked.

"I'm fine. I didn't even have a chance to take a sip. This idiot on the other hand ..."

"You know what I mean. You better call me when you get home."

Faith nodded and raised the window, looking both ways pulling out of the driveway, but a car sped around the blind spot, nearly hitting them. Frank shouted, startling both kids, making them cry. "We're okay Honey Bunches," she assured them. "Mommy had plenty of time."

Faith stopped at the end of the street, out of sight from the house. "This is stopping. Now."

"What?"

"Calm down." She warned.

She took the diamond earrings out of her ears and tossed them in the cup holder rubbing her lobes. She couldn't remember the last time she'd taken them off since their wedding. She tried not to inhale the stench of vomit, barley and veggie dip emanating from his breath. "We will talk about this when we get home," she whispered, peeking back to see if little Miss Astute was watching. She was; her eyes wide. "Right now I need to get you coffee."

"I'm fine."

"You're not."

Jenna fell asleep by the time they got to the drive-thru so there was no whining for a strawberry frosted donut with sprinkles. Back on the road a sharp wail came from the back.

"Frank, turn around and put Kyle's pacifier in his mouth."

"I can't."

"What do you mean you can't?"

He started to hyperventilate.

"You mean you won't even try." Faith sighed. She fumbled to find it resting near Kyle's tummy while she drove, but it must have fallen under him so she needed to pull over into the commuter lot across the street, almost passing it. She screeched to make the turn, nearly clipping the fence post at the entrance. She smashed the brakes to a halt.

Jenna stirred.

Frank smashed his cup in the holder. "You're gonna make me spill it."

She paused to question him. “There’s a top on it, what are you talking about?” She reached back, found the pacifier, and popped it in Kyle’s mouth appeasing him. “How easy was that? You couldn’t do that?”

Frank remained silent.

“What happened to AA, Frank? What happened to your sponsor?”

“I can have one.”

Faith’s eyes widened. “Are you kidding me? One what? One beer?” She paused. “Absolutely not. You’ve proven that over and over.”

“I don’t know what you’re talking about.” He slurped from the cup.

“Exactly the problem.”

A second later, Frank screamed and flailed around like he was covered in spiders. He flung the door open and jumped out of the car, tossing the cup several parking spaces away.

Faith yelled at him through his open door. “What the hell is your problem?”

“It was leaking.”

“Why would it be leaking?” She thought for a brief second and gasped. She fished through the puddle of hot French Vanilla in the center console, pulling out one single diamond earring. The emergency brake glitched when she yanked on it, and her seat belt trapped her in before she fought her way out. She sprang out of the car and ran toward the broken styrofoam in the parking lot, pushing Frank out of the way. Falling to her hands and knees, she scraped the gravel with her fingers. “It’s a sign. It’s a sign.”

“What’s a sign? What are you doing?”

"My earring." Faith could hardly speak. "I can't find it."

Frank belched and stumbled back to the front seat of the car.

"You aren't going to help me find it?" She cried.

Frank didn't budge. But when a light flashed over from a car entering the commuter lot, Frank freaked out. "Get in the car," he barked.

"I'm looking for my earring."

"Hurry."

"What is *wrong* with you?"

"There's a cop. Get in the car. Quick" He demanded.

"Who cares? We're not doing anything wrong."

"I've been drinking."

"So? You're not the one driving, calm down."

The officer looped in and out of the lot but Faith was not his priority either. She scanned the pavement for a hint of sparkle but the darkness enveloped her and she couldn't see past it. The tears started and continued the rest of the way home. The disregard. The addiction. Why couldn't he stay sober for himself, for his family? That was the last chance Frank had left. The last chance Faith had in her to give. She couldn't help him. She couldn't make him do it. He'd caused a scene in front of the people she loved the most when up until then she'd done a pretty good job hiding it, she thought. Their happy family. Their perfect little life. Two perfect children; a boy and girl. A cute little house. But she wasn't happy. She hadn't been for what felt like forever. And nothing would change. How could she keep expecting it to? She'd chosen this life with him. She couldn't make him happy. She'd failed.

When they arrived home, Frank collapsed into his recliner; leaving Faith to take three trips carrying bags and half-sleeping children from the driveway. She settled Kyle down in the crib after trying to force two ounces of his bottle and when she returned to the living room, Jenna had taken it upon herself to console Frank who was still worried about the officer in the commuter lot. Faith had no idea what was going on. Sweat poured from his brow and he struggled to breathe, even without a child sitting on his chest trying to "take care of him".

"Get her off of me," he said between belches.

"Daddy sick?" Jenna said.

"Yes, honey, daddy is sick." Faith hissed at Frank. "He just doesn't think he is or that it has any effect on the rest of us." She whispered at him. She reached for Jenna's hand for bedtime.

Frank was still in the same condition on the recliner when Faith returned. "When are you going to shape up and get some help because I'm done. I'm done trying to help if you're not going to help yourself. AA was a complete joke." Her eyes widened. "You never called a sponsor, did you? Her heart sank with his silence. "Give me his name." Giving him another chance. "That's what I thought."

Faith downloaded divorce papers that night after the kids went to bed.

"What are you doing?" He barged in snatching the papers.

"Printing divorce papers."

"Yeah, okay," he mocked.

"Yeah, okay is right," she mimicked his tone.

He stood and stared, not understanding the problem.

"How about a Counselor? Marriage counseling."

"We don't need counseling."

"It's that or divorce," she warned.

"Fine." He agreed, only to appease the crazy woman who was blowing things out of proportion and not serious about divorcing him.

- 9 -

A week later, Faith went looking for Frank around the house for their marriage counselor appointment. "I can't find him anywhere," she said to Dianna into the phone.

"I'm on my way anyway so I can help knock some sense into him for you when you find him. Speaking of sense, why are you doing this, Faith?"

"Doing what?"

"You *know* what. Marriage counseling."

"I want my kids to know that I did everything I could to save this marriage. This divorce is not my fault."

"No one said it is, or that you have to endure him in the meantime. You're going to stroke out being on this rollercoaster all the time with him."

"I want out Dianna, I do. I just want to make sure."

Dianna paused for a long minute. "I love you and I'll be here for you. But you've given him too many chances to change. He won't change."

Faith noticed that the garage door was open and found Frank hiding the largest beer can she'd ever seen behind a gallon of old paint hidden in front of her car. She would never have known it was there if she didn't see him put it there. "I found him." Faith told Dianna.

"Ok, see you in a minute."

"Are you kidding me right now Frank? A tallboy? We have an appointment."

"When?"

Faith rolled her eyes.

"Look, we don't need a divorce or counseling," he begged. "It won't happen again."

"How many times have you said that? You're doing it right now. Do you think I'm an idiot? You need someone knocking the booze out of your hand when you don't have the brains enough to stop? Not anymore. Go ahead. Choose alcohol. Drink yourself into oblivion. Drive yourself into a tree. But it won't be on my watch."

"You're overreacting."

"How many times have you been drunk since Dianna's?" Frank didn't respond. "Too many," she continued. "You're making this family miserable and you don't even realize it."

"Yeah, okay," he repeated, condescension oozing from his voice.

"Dianna will be here soon to watch the kids."

"You told Dianna?" His face grew disappointed. Not in what he'd done, but in that other people knew his secret.

"Did you think the kids were coming with us? What is wrong with you? Frank, you need help. We need help. This marriage is falling apart and you don't even see it. The appointment is in two hours, get dressed."

"I don't appreciate you telling everyone our business."

"You negated that when you decided to have a drunken rage in front of MY friends and our kids at Dianna's house. I'm done hiding this for you. I'll be at the counselor's appointment with or without you. And I'm taking my own car. Alone."

Faith stepped inside the counselor's office and was greeted by the therapist himself. *How nice it must be to hang a shingle from your porch and commute to the other room.* She daydreamed sinking into the buttery couch, looking at all the credentials and books on the shelves when Frank showed up. Her body tensed. She'd already accepted the fact that he wouldn't show up and that she'd be divorcing him. He chose alcohol over the family and didn't want help, yet there he was sitting next to her.

Frank and Faith divulged their grievances, talking over each other. Frank corrected and dismissed Faith's feelings. She began to shut down, used to it. Frank admitted that he treated everyone equally. "I don't discriminate. I do it to everyone. I've lived this way my entire life. I don't change." He laughed like it was a big joke.

She stopped the tears from falling. Anger set in. The therapist took a long sigh and put his hand up, stopping the toxic dialogue between them. After digging down and exposing the bare bones of each of their childhoods, he told her she'd been living some form of this all her life, so marrying Frank, "a spoiled man-child", was familiar to her.

Frank's jaw muscles tightened.

Faith thought for a long while not knowing what to say. "I never knew it had a name. My whole life, everything was always my fault, my problem, I was always the difficult person to get along with. Always."

The therapist handed Faith another tissue. "Look," he said. "The tension between you is palpable. You are broken. Frank, you have a problem and aren't willing to fix it. Faith," he continued, "you run the household with no break or help. You enable him by doing it all so Frank doesn't have to; making bottles at all hours of the night, cleaning the vomit, going with him to AA, not expecting him to go to any doctor's appointments. I will say … that you have had to lighten up on the rare occasion that Frank buys the green toothpaste instead of the blue…" Faith fidgeted. "But you need to compromise." He turned to Frank who was looking at something out the window. "Frank, stop complaining about how many spoons Faith leaves in the sink and be grateful you have a cooked meal. Maybe tell her she's doing a good job, take a night shift with the baby. Cook something. Bring home a pizza. Take Jenna to the park so Faith can nap when Kyle naps. Faith, maybe try to use less spoons." Faith smiled at his attempt at a joke. "But in the end, it's not about any of that. It's about communication. It's about trust. It's about being there for each other and being accountable. If something you're doing is hurting the other and they've told you that it bothers them but you keep doing that exact thing … that should make you want to stop, right?" He waited for Frank to respond.

"I guess so." Frank admitted.

Faith stopped a tear from trickling down her cheek and chewed her lip.

"In the end," the therapist said, "it's about how many chances does one get in order to change? So, Faith…" he handed her the box of tissues and the wastepaper basket, "do you have any more chances left in you and..." He turned to Frank, "Do you want to stay in the marriage and can you work on some things to get help, to get sober?" These were as much statements as they were questions. "I'm willing to help, whatever the decision. But the decision is yours and only yours to make. Together. If you want this to work."

Faith wrung her hands in her lap. She'd already made the decision to divorce him. She really didn't want to make anything else work. She was done. But for the sake of the kids, she would see if there was anything at all that could make things better. "Yes," she squeaked out her answer.

"And," Frank hesitated, "I will go back to AA."

They scheduled their follow up visit for the following two weeks.

They had all woken up that Sunday an hour later than usual, which was the rest that Faith needed. Spring previewed its beauty and the birds sang songs of hope outside the window. For the first time in a long while, they had no plans and Faith enjoyed the peace with a steaming cup of tea. A bee buzzed by in the sunshine.

Faith heard a little fussing from the back room, but was pleased that Frank was on changing duty and for the first time in a while she could sit and enjoy a full cup of hot tea. *He didn't drink yesterday.* She thought. Jenna knew the exact outfit she wanted to wear so Faith knew the changing session would be easy. Thud. Faith jumped, spilling some tea on the sill. She ran toward Jenna's room.

"Daddy punch wall," Jenna tattled. His tongue was sticking out, letting out a piercing squeal, his signature tantrum.

"Are you ok?" She asked Jenna, brushing past Frank, scooping Jenna up from the changing table, caressing her head and cradling her to her breast like an infant. "Is she ok? Did you hurt her?" She hissed.

His response was delayed. "No, of course not."

"Then … *what* are you doing?"

"Daddy hit wall, daddy hit wall," Jenna continued.

"She kicked me in the face."

Faith turned before he could answer. While in the doorway, she stopped to look back. "Are you drunk?" She whispered.

"No."

"Well, what's the problem then? You know what? This isn't working," Faith warned. "I'm done."

"Well … you want this divorce, not me." His voice trailed after her down the hallway until he caught up.

"That's for sure," she said under her breath.

Frank was standing closer than she expected when she turned around after putting Jenna down. She stepped back.

"I'm not drunk." He said.

"So what's the problem? Why are you so angry? Can you call your sponsor?"

"I'm fine."

"Okay…" she stepped closer, not smelling alcohol. "But you're on edge and it's getting worse. Having a fit? Hitting a wall in front of our children? This has got to stop. And if you won't talk to me, maybe you can talk to *someone.*"

Frank reached for his phone and left the room. A few minutes later, he headed toward the door. "I'm going to meet my sponsor."

Faith breathed a sigh of relief. She'd watched him walk out that door a thousand times but even though he was acting up, he wasn't drinking. This time. He was trying. Faith could see how hard it was for him. He left the house before she could tell him she was glad he was doing something about it. She cleaned the house while she waited and scrubbed a bit harder as the hours passed. She hated that she always expected him to disappoint her, but based on his history, he always did. He was meeting his sponsor, what did she have to worry about? He wouldn't be sitting at the bar alone this time. He wouldn't be at the bar at all. He needed his sponsor.

Several hours later, Faith picked up her phone to call Frank, but put it back down more than once. She scrolled through the texts. No text. She checked on the kids, again. She looked at the time; four hours, five hours. "Where are you?" That was the first text. "This is my third message. Call me back." "Where are you? Text me back." She noticed the sponsor's card on the table and flipped it in her fingers. She dialed the first few digits on the card, stopping herself each time she tried to call until the six-hour mark. "I called your sponsor. You never called him. Call me back. Now." There was no answer.

Faith put the kids in the car and drove around town. It didn't take long to find Frank's car in the coat factory parking lot across a double-lined road; the perfect hiding place for men who didn't want their wives to know they frequented the only strip club in town. She parked her car in plain view next to his and called him. "Where are you?"

"I went for a drive down the parkway."

"Where are you now?"

"I'm a few towns over."

"Really." It wasn't a question.

"What?" His word drawn out.

"I'm looking at you right now." Before he registered what she had said, he shuffled past the hood of her car and their eyes met in slow motion. He didn't stop. He didn't acknowledge the importance of the situation until she mouthed, "It's over" through the windshield and sped away while Jenna screamed for her daddy. Faith debated on anonymously calling 911 for a drunk driver in the neighborhood but wanted to get the kids home before he got there, preventing more trauma.

"What the hell Frank?" She caught him outside before entering the house. She daydreamed that she'd had the courage to double-bolt the lock or beat him in the head with a bat.

"I didn't know what else to do."

"What else to do? Seriously? Play with your kids. Let me take a nap. Take them to the park, go for a walk. Mow the lawn. Call your sponsor. Do something! But sitting in the dark, in the middle of the day, at a strip club … alone? It's disgusting and disrespectful. This is over. I'm done." Faith couldn't listen to any more it-won't-happen-agains. But this time he couldn't even say that. He staggered to the recliner.

Faith showed up alone to their second marriage counseling session and stood in the doorway of the office, gaining the courage to go in. She used to be happy. Strong. She could hardly remember it. Before marriage. Before kids. Before meeting Frank for that matter. Fragile. Terrorized by his tone, his words. Wondering if he'd come home alive or in cuffs, behind the wheel in a daze, secretly hoping he wouldn't show up.

"So the question is," the therapist started, "what do you want for yourself Faith?"

Faith didn't have to think before answering. "My health. My happiness. What am I teaching my daughter by staying with a man who doesn't respect me? He ruins every SINGLE happy moment of our entire lives and he won't get help."

"That's on him. You've done all you can do. And when his fist hit that wall, that could have been the beginning or the end."

"I know."

"Did you have clues along the way that could have helped you make the right decision choosing him as a partner?"

"No. He was always sweet."

"Where did you meet again?"

Faith scrunched her nose. She knew the therapist was right. Frank had become progressively drunk the night they met, but he told her that he never usually drank, so she believed him. Faith was used to people needing a beer to take the edge off or in order to fall asleep. She loved listening to her grandfather crack open an icy beer on a hot summer morning, the swoosh, the fizz, the gulp, the sigh … the burp. It was the preparation for every project, every day. Nights ended sitting on the couch in a stained undershirt watching whatever game was on the "tube" with another cold beer. Faith was the designated beer-getter, trained to get him a beer whenever he was near the end of one. *But he was never drunk.* She thought. He drank his beer like water. Morning, noon, and night.

Faith gasped. "I never realized." Faith told the therapist while looking off into the distance. She thought about Frank passed out in the recliner in her living room, she thought about watching her grandmother shoving slabs of bread at her grandfather "to sop up the alcohol". Watching her grandmother roll her eyes whenever he called her a "Bitch", letting his insults roll off of her, but sending Faith to hide behind the yellow chair, scared. Faith knitted her brows.

The therapist interrupted. "Tell me about when your children were born."

"Oh man," Faith pressed her fingers into her forehead and exhaled. The details flooded her brain like a tsunami. Shaking her head, she remembered what should have been another happy moment in their marriage. "He didn't want to pick us up."

Faith saw the therapist react ever so slightly. He lowered his head to write on his yellow pad while she recalled the story. She didn't hear the scribbling of his notes because her mind relived the moment as if it had been yesterday.

Faith carried her newborn like a football in the crook of her arm. Swaddled in a striped bundle, he couldn't have been more content to be held. She waited for Frank to answer her call. He didn't pick up the first time. "Guess what? We're ready to come home!" She waited for his response and the excitement drained from her face. "Yes, now," she squinted at the phone to look at the time, shaking her head. "You knew that would be today."

After ending the call. "Let's wait for daddy on the bed." She talked to Kyle in soothing tones." She held her stomach to provide some relief from her new wound and climbed into the bed with Kyle to wait. After days in the Neonatal Intensive Care Unit, Kyle was ready to go home and Faith couldn't wait to have cuddle time with Jenna and their complete family.

Faith snuggled next to him and felt the shape of his head under the blue beanie that kept him warm even though it was September and the cool weather hadn't arrived yet. "My son," she whispered. "I'm going to do everything I can to teach you how to be a decent man. With every part of me, I promise you." Kyle opened his eyes and looked at her as if he understood and would hold her to that. She couldn't help it but her eyes welled up. "Aw, come here." She pulled him in and pressed her nose into his face. Her heart leapt while she breathed in his newborn scent plus baby shampoo. She wasn't sure how she could love another thing as much as her first child until this little guy came into her life. She smiled when she rubbed her lips against his peach-fuzz forehead, the same thing she loved doing to Jenna. She estimated that she had given him a thousand kisses all over already, at least. His black eyelashes were already long and tickled her cheek when she rested her face there. They both fell asleep before Kyle stirred, wanting to eat again. She tried to sit up, holding her stomach.

A quick knock at the door startled her. An orderly whispered, "Can I take this wheelchair? I'll bring it right back."

"Sure but I'm getting picked up soon, I need to have this wheelchair back quickly."

"Is your ride here?" The orderly looked around.

"I don't know where he is." Faith looked at the time.

"Okay ... well ... I'll return it right away."

Faith nodded and Kyle started to fuss. "Come here kiddo." Faith fed him the same special formula that he drank through the feeding tube in the NICU. Now he was able to drink on his own but he had trouble sucking. She held him sitting up so he didn't take in too much air but was soon cleaning up the projectile vomit.

"Mama." Jenna ran in and climbed into bed for hugs and kisses.

"Jenna-Jenna, I love you so much. I missed you."

"I la uooo too, mama."

"Let's go," Frank bellowed, "I thought you were ready."

"Shhh!" Faith hushed. "We were, but –" Faith started to explain.

"You should have been ready." Frank interrupted.

"Kyle was hungry again. He's almost done."

Frank paced the cramped room, hands flailing, grumbling.

"Plus we need to wait for the orderly with the wheel-

chair," Faith added.

"What wheelchair? You have legs. You can walk."

Faith shot him a look. His apathy shocked her every time, crushing her, but her priority was her babies, not Frank. Faith glanced toward Jenna to see if she was paying attention. She was. She always was. Faith pursed her lips and whispered. "What is your problem Frank?" Faith stepped closer to him and caught a whiff of beer. "Have you been drinking?"

"Don't worry about it," he said with a drawl.

"I la uooo Brudder," Jenna interrupted and said to Kyle, kissing his face.

Faith turned to Jenna. "Oh honey, what a great big sister you are." Jenna snuck Kyle's pacifier into her mouth when no one was looking. "Did you have fun with daddy?"

Before Jenna had a chance to answer, Kyle threw up onto the drop cloth that was waiting. Jenna sprang up on the bed, shouting, "Ewe" and tried to fling herself over the rail.

"Frank." Faith reached out to grab Jenna, but winced and held her stomach from pain. "Get her before she falls out."

"Why do we have to wait for a wheelchair? I don't understand why you just can't walk."

"The next time you have your stomach cut open, I won't have any empathy for you either. Besides, it's hospital rule, I need to be wheeled out."

"No it isn't." Frank mocked.

Faith rolled her eyes.

"Knock-Knock. Someone ready to go home?" The overly cheerful orderly clapped his hands together at the

sight of the beautiful family in front of him, not knowing what he was stepping into.

Faith was wheeled over to the pick-up area. As per her extensive birth plan, it was time to have some mommy-and-me time with Jenna and Frank was to carry Kyle to the car in the parking garage and drive around to pick them up. But Jenna wasn't having it. She threw a fit and whined for Frank to pick her up and carry her to the car.

"Frank, it's okay, please just bring Jenna to the car. I'll wait here with Kyle."

"No, you're coming with us."

"I can barely walk, you expect me to walk to the escalator, across the bridge to the parking garage elevator and then to find the car?"

"Yes."

Faith held her stomach in while she walked to a chair, wincing with pain. Kyle snuggled asleep in his car seat missing the whole show. Frank plunked Kyle down by her feet. "Watch it," she scolded.

Frank huffed out of the hospital with the two-year old in his arms. Faith rocked the baby carrier with her foot letting him know she was there.

A while later, Frank pulled in and parked in the circular driveway in front of her, but he didn't come out of the car. She could see him waiting for her. He waited. Faith waited. They stared at each other through the glass wall of windows.

Faith reached down to lift the baby in the carrier but pain shot through her belly. The carrier didn't budge. She sat back up, clutching her stomach. Frank got out of the car and stood next to it a while longer until storming through the doors in a whirlwind of nasty, Jenna in his arms. He scolded Faith as if she were a child that had done something wrong. "What are you doing?" he yelled in front of visitors, staff, and security.

Faith couldn't string her words together quickly enough to answer him. He whisked Kyle up in the carrier, whirling him around. He bent down abducting the toddler in his other arm and fled out the door. He was already back at the car before Faith could get out of the chair. She attempted to get up, but the pain stabbed her again and forced her to sit back down. Defeat turned to disappointment, her head slumped and she brushed tears from her face. Several minutes later, she shook her head, tried to get out of the chair and padded toward the car.

Frank fumed, trying several times to lock the baby carrier into place before succeeding. Faith brushed her fingers over the handle of the passenger door, trying to figure out a pain-free way to pull the door open. Frank watched from the driver side. Faith waited for him to come over. Frank plodded over to her side, she thought, to open the door. She stepped back gingerly to let him do so, but he stepped back too, as if to force her to open it herself; she was, after all, there first. A standoff occurred. He groaned and tilted his head back like a child. He opened the door but that was it. He was already heading to the driver's side.

Faith made her way into the front seat.

"Where were you and why did it take so long to get in the car?" He yelled.

Faith froze. This stranger, her husband, a bully. His words, intimidating actions, selfishness exploded, stabbing her over and over. The feeling cemented, never to be forgotten.

Frank started the car and rolled an inch.

"My door."

"What about it?"

"My door is open."

"So shut it." He said.

For a split second, she reached toward the door but grabbed her stomach, clutching her stitches. "I can't." Her voice died in her throat.

Frank jammed the brakes and threw the car in park, giving her the evil eye. He pin-balled around to her side jamming his thigh into the front bumper. He slammed her door shut nearly toppling himself over. When he got back to the driver's side Faith tried to focus on him but he was a blur through the tears that she willed not to fall. She whispered so Jenna couldn't hear. "What the hell is your problem? I can't walk. I can't lift. I couldn't even get out of the chair. You act like we've never done this before." Faith waited.

He hung his head and sighed. "I forgot," he said, almost apologetically.

"Of course you did. You know what? No. Even if you did forget, can you see that I'm uncomfortable right now? It's never been about me. It's always been about you. You couldn't care less about anyone else but yourself. You're treating me like crap," she struggled to get the words out.

"You're too sensitive."

"Really? Because you're being a jerk and you're ruining this for me."

"You are wrong."

"Really? This was a moment I had imagined my entire life. Bringing our son home with our daughter, a complete family. Pretend to be a proud father and hus-

band, for God's Sake."

Faith tried to turn and look back at her children. Jenna was staring at her brother with love. "My brudder."

"Yes baby, your brother."

Faith looked forward. The dam broke free and her tears streamed down. The picture Faith had imagined all her life of this moment, holding hands, in love with her sweet husband driving carefully with his precious cargo in the car crashed down when the tire hit the curb, Faith held her stomach cringing and Frank peeled out of the lot.

Minutes later he was on the recliner watching the end of the Red Sox game with a beer and Faith was still trying to get in the house.

The counselor interrupted her thoughts. "So Faith…"

She bit her lip, focusing back on him, wiping real tears from her face she didn't realize were falling.

"You marry your unfinished business."

Faith thought about it for a minute.

He continued. "Your whole life you've wanted to be seen, to be heard, to be appreciated, to be loved. When Frank came along, it was all too familiar. You didn't know he was like your mother, but subconsciously, you did. And this time you thought you'd be able to change it. But instead, you're still trying to fit in to what someone else deems convenient without taking your own feelings into consideration. It's the way you allow Frank to live the way he does. It's the way your father deals with your mother. It's the way your grandmother handled your grandfather. Those were not model relationships, but you never knew anything different. It's time Faith. It's time for you to be happy and figure out what you want. It's time you got a break. It's time to get off the rollercoaster. The eggshells, the day-to-day stress. The breadcrumbs. It's breaking you."

Faith accepted the tissue that the therapist handed her and sobbed for the death of her marriage, grieving a life she wished for, happiness she'd never have if she stayed with Frank. He chose alcohol over his family, and time proved that again and again. Faith knew what she needed to do. It was time to stop being a pawn in the game. Her words mattered. Her feelings mattered.

"Faith, you've been conditioned your entire life to think that everything was your fault; that if your mother was upset that it was because of you. That if Frank has to go spend his paycheck at the bar it's because you used three spoons instead of two. When Frank causes a scene in the middle of a store, you immediately remember your mother doing the same thing. It's okay for Frank to get in the car and drive away because that's what people do, that's what your mother did, leaving you home alone to take care of your siblings, to take care of everything. It isn't always your fault.

"Wow." Faith hadn't thought about it that way before. *You marry your unfinished business.* "I guess the breadcrumbs he leaves for me to hang on to aren't working anymore."

"They never were. You've been sucked into the hope that people change. That he will change. But without trying, he won't. In fact, he's told you that himself."

Faith gathered her things and thanked the doctor.

"Faith, Frank has to *want* to make you happy. Even knowing that he's doing something that makes you upset, he still does it. That shows that he doesn't truly care about your feelings."

"Maybe I am too sensitive."

"Faith, your feelings are not right or wrong. It's how you feel. Never justify that. To anyone."

Faith dabbed her nose with the tissue unable to speak. She knew what she had to do.

"Are you okay to drive?"

She nodded. "It's all so clear now."

-10-

Frank continued sneaking around even after he promised to change, but Faith was no longer surprised. She grew to expect it. The thoughts, *"He'll never change,"* repeated in her head. "I can't live like this anymore." She ate the last forkful from her plate and stared at Frank's empty chair near her at the table, his meal untouched. She heard rustling and clanging near the bedroom. "For God's sake, what now?" She ran up the stairs. He froze, trying to block her. She pushed through. Frank shoved a large black trash bag into the darkness of the cubby. The more he tried to hide the full bag of bottles and cans, the louder it rattled.

"This is ridiculous Frank. You're not even trying." *He's never going to change.* Faith thought. She smacked her hands on her hips. *Why do I keep expecting him to?* She walked down the stairs shaking her head, hearing the cans rattling in the background. *What am I going to do? Can I do this on my own? Can I survive being married to him? I need a sign.* Lightning crackled above the house, startling her. *Is this my sign? What should I do?* She whispered.

Faith wanted to finish the laundry before the storm hit

but it was already upon them. Jenna got scared when the thunder hit, so she tended to her first. Rain smashed down in buckets against the house. Faith pulled a cozy blanket over them and started to read Jenna a book. She sighed with contentment when Frank barged in. "What are you doing? I want to watch the game."

"We're reading."

"I thought you were doing laundry."

"You can do laundry too," Faith snapped, knowing the conversation wasn't going to go anywhere. "Jenna, honey, your dad wants to watch TV, can you go set up something in your room for us to play while Mommy gets the laundry from the basement?" Jenna skipped out of the room without being asked twice. Frank belched and propped his feet up on the recliner with a large cup of soda in hand, but Faith knew he'd already had his share of alcohol or that it was actually in the cup. She checked on Kyle and made her way downstairs.

"Oh my God," Faith ran down a few steps and stopped. "Frank, get down here right now." He didn't answer. "Frank! Get down here, it's an emergency."

"Why?" He took his time to arrive on the scene. He pushed past her on the stairs. "What did you do?"

"I didn't do this."

"Well you were doing laundry."

"I didn't cause this. It's not the washer, the rain must have come in somehow." Muddy water splashed onto the bottom step. Toys and half empty detergent containers bobbed in half a foot of rising water. He turned halfway back up the staircase, grabbing the banister like a child afraid of the stairs falling in.

"Frank, what should we do?"

"How am I supposed to know?" He snapped back.

They both stared at the damage. A large white box floated by and she gasped.

"What?"

She knew its contents instantly. Pearl beads, delicate lace … "My gown. It's ruined."

"What gown?"

"My wedding gown." She pressed her hands into her temples. "It's a sign." She repeated over and over.

"What's a sign?" Frank grumbled something else under his breath.

"It's destroyed," she whispered.

Seconds later, the front door slammed and she heard the pitch of Frank's car reversing out of the driveway. She slumped down onto the final three steps and buried her face in her hands. Rocking herself to comfort, she felt like a sad child again, listening to her mother peel off into the distance, not knowing when or if she would be back. Would she be mad or happy when she returned? It felt the same every time Frank left her. Alone. Mad.

After she soaked up the last of her tears with her sleeve, she stared into the brown river swirling below. "It's truly over," she said. "In every way."

Days later, after the water table subsided, Faith was still cleaning up the mess. She swept the last of the puddles toward the sump pump, leaving the final pile to sort and wring out. She dug out a glass trinket box engraved with their names and wedding date in swirls, flower buds and fancy font. The cover creaked when she opened it, but the velvet inside seemed intact. She turned the box over to inspect it when one of the glass panels slid out, crashing to the ground. Her fingers trembled when she tried to fit their names back together but it was irreparable. "That's my sign," she repeated. She gripped the glass tighter before smashing it at the wall. "That's. It." She raced through the pile and flung every memento against the cement; her bouquet, votive candles, a box of wedding shoes. When she was sure that her wedding memories were obliterated, she stormed up the stairs to reprint the missing divorce papers and find a mediator.

Hours later, Frank entered the house, staggering.

Faith winced. "I found a mediator," she said. "I have an estimate on how much it would cost and as long as we don't drag it out, we should be able to split the cost and proceed."

"I didn't think you were serious." Frank stared.

Faith shrugged. "You've had your warnings and you've done nothing to help yourself. Or me. So you're the one who wasn't serious about changing. And, to be honest, I never thought you would."

"Yeah, okay."

"Keep it up Frank. You're fucking making this easy on me."

The chill in her tone surprised him. He'd never heard her swear. "You think this is easy for me?" He searched for whatever words he could to hang on. "What if I had cancer? Would you leave me then?" He grasped for a lifeline.

"Frank," She sighed. Her voice softened and her shoulders fell. "That's not fair. If you had cancer, you'd get help. But you do have a cancer. You have an addiction and you're not getting help. You're making it miserable to live with you. And you're making my decision easier with each new incident."

"I told you it wouldn't happen again."

"But it does. And it always will."

"Nice that you don't trust me."

"You've had your chances."

"Well, it must be nice to be so perfect that you don't need anything or do anything wrong. Well, I'm sorry. I'm not perfect like you."

Faith squinted. "All you need is to get help."

"It's not as bad as you think."

"That's the problem, Frank. It is. And you don't see it. And, yes, that's my answer. I want a divorce."

"Kyle's sick again. I need to bring him back to the pediatrician. Something's wrong. He's pretty lethargic and warm but I don't think it's an ear infection. Can you please help me bring Jenna to the sitter?"

"I have to work."

"Please bring her, it's on your way."

Frank stared blankly as if bringing her was completely out of the question.

"Fine, Faith said, "I'll bring her with me." The less interaction she had in order to keep the peace with Frank the better, she thought. He wasn't making sense. He wasn't doing what he needed to help her so he might as well go to work on time, proving his dependability with the outside world.

Kyle's vitals were checked upon arrival and before

they were settled in the exam room, Faith saw the pediatrician approaching them.

"You need to get Kyle to the hospital. Now."

"What? Um … I? What's wrong?"

"I'm not sure, but his temperature is too high."

Faith was trying to figure out what the doctor was saying, but she was interrupted.

"You need to go now. Go straight there and do not stop."

Faith's heart raced. She called Frank on the way telling him she needed his help with Jenna while she swayed over the lines on the highway and horns honked. Faith swerved back into her lane. Jenna screamed from the backseat. Faith couldn't concentrate. Why did Kyle have to go to the hospital? Driving with one hand, Frank in the other ear asking questions that Faith didn't know the answer to. She could barely hear him. He couldn't understand her words between her hyperventilation. She hung up thinking he would meet her at the emergency department.

Hours after paperwork and tests that required blood work were finished, still no one knew why Kyle was sick. They waited. Minutes ticked by. Jenna was getting impatient. Frank eventually showed, finding them quarantined in a corner room with windows. He gasped when he saw Kyle hooked up to all the tubes and wires, backing himself out into the hallway where Faith could see him pacing. Everyone did. The room was like sitting in a fishbowl, easily accessible for viewing by specialists.

Jenna followed him out and Frank picked her up, parading her around the hallway in her little doctor gown and hair net, asking nurses for paper and pens so she had something to draw on. This charade lasted another twenty-minutes before he finally masked up with gloves and gown to enter the room so as not to contract *whatever* it was that Kyle had. Viral or bacterial? No one knew. But every doctor and visitor had to follow the infectious disease protocols and rules until they figured out what was going on. He entered the room and barraged Faith with questions she still didn't know the answers to.

Frank's parents flew in to help with Jenna so Frank could go to work or pop in and out of the hospital as he pleased. Each time, he hesitated at Kyle's door, unable to process his emotions, unable to step inside right away.

"What are you doing Frank?"

"I … I can't see him like this."

"You're not here."

"What if he dies, Faith?"

"Frank. What if he lives? What will his life be like? Will he walk? Will he talk? We don't know. I need you to be present."

"I can't." He started pacing, making her nervous.

"Look, I'm worried about him too. But what are we going to do? Right now, I need you to take a shift. I need rest."

"I have to go to work." Frank started toward the door.

"You just got here." Her voice trailed after him. Faith was too tired to argue. She'd been watching the numbers on the monitors for days without answers. She'd watched Kyle's lips turn blue every time his oxygen levels fell. How many times did a nurse tell her she needed a break; to leave and get a good night's sleep in her own bed? She'd been standing vigil at Kyle's bed, rubbing his head and talking to him all week, barely sleeping or eating.

The ring on her phone interrupted her thoughts and it gave her an excuse to sit for the first time all week. Kyle's body looked so tiny and helpless through the bars on the bed. She kept an eye on him while she talked. "Yeah," she told her boss on the other end of the phone. "I'll be there. I'm looking forward to coming back to work and seeing everyone," she told him.

"We miss you," her boss said.

"Aw, I miss you all too. Yeah sure, I can do that. I can't wait." They made a plan of what she would be doing when she returned even though she couldn't think of anything else but Kyle in that moment. "It was a tough road with this little guy," she admitted. "Lots of appointments."

"Yeah," her boss agreed. "I heard that."

Faith wondered who told him. "Yeah, but he'll be fine."

"Of course." Her boss paused. "I remember we were in the office and you were keeping track of contractions before we sent you home and the doctors put you on bed rest."

"Yeah, he thought he was done brewing."

"Wasn't that two months early?"

"Don't remind me!" Faith chuckled. "But don't worry. Won't happen again." Faith looked forward to going back to work and planning her escape from Frank. She didn't tell her boss about any of it, especially that she was in the hospital with Kyle at that very moment.

By the end of the week, deliriously tired, she took the nurse's advice to get out of the hospital, make a hair cut appointment, spend time with Jenna and sleep in her own bed. But within minutes of making the appointment, she felt guilty for wanting to leave Kyle, for taking the time to care for herself. *How can I go and have a good night's sleep and get my hair done when he's in the hospital and we don't know what's wrong with him?* But she called Frank and told him about her plans for the next day. "Please be here at 7am so I can go home and take a real shower and maybe take a short nap before my appointment." She was shocked that he had agreed.

Seven thirty and seven forty-five came and went the following morning. She chewed more of the inside of her cheek with each passing minute, pacing back and forth to her packed bag, looking into the small stand up shower with the safety handle, waiting for Kyle to start demanding his next two ounce feeding. After a particularly disruptive night of doctors entering the room at all hours, she squinted with bloodshot eyes when the eight o'clock hour rang in and the hospital enlivened. Fluorescent lights flicked on in the hallway, nurses and maintenance workers talked and laughed loudly, breakfast utensils clinked, intercoms blared, buzzers, alarms, phones rang, welcoming a new day. And no sign of Frank.

"I thought you were going home," the day nurse said while preparing to sign onto her shift.

The sight of her brought on a flood of emotion. The nurse had left the night before, went home to sleep, now she was back. It was a new day. *An entirely new day.* Time was passing by and Faith was standing still. She watched the nurse write the names of Kyle's daytime staff on the white board by the door. "Frank was supposed to be here so I could leave. He's taking away from my time. It's *my* time." She repeated.

The nurse saw Faith's lip quiver and the tears were

about to flow. "Go." She rushed her toward the shower. "Take a shower. I'll watch Kyle."

"You don't have to do that."

"Girl, you need a break. It's the least I can do. I have a few minutes before I have to make my rounds."

Faith obliged. She turned the shower on and waited for it to get as hot as it would get. The pump soap on the wall smelled extra medicinally and when the shampoo didn't rinse out of her greasy hair, she grunted, trying not to break down. All she wanted was one shower at home and a few hour break. She wanted to cuddle up with Jenna because that would make it all better.

By the time Frank showed up, Faith was balled up in the corner of the walk-in shower. She pressed her fingers deep into her face to muffle her sobbing. The drops trickled from the showerhead, and she shivered. The nurse let herself out and Frank banged on the bathroom door with expletives. "What are you doing in there?"

Faith rushed to dry off, talking to him through the door. "You were supposed to be here." She said, holding back the tears. "Where were you?"

"I was tired. I slept in." Frank shrugged.

Faith wailed and Frank hushed her. "You only think about yourself," Faith began. "I've been up all night for a week. Literally standing over his crib day and night. I miss Jenna. I wanted a little bit of time and you've taken that away from me."

"I'm here, aren't I?" He jiggled the door handle.

Her eyes widened. "I wanted to take a shower at home and spend time with Jenna before my appointment and now I only have time to go straight there."

"Well, you need to bring the car back by twelve because I told my parents they could take your car to meet my brother at Chili's."

"Wait. WHAT? I have to rush back because you made plans for them to take my car? Have them take yours."

"I'm going to meet them there from here." Frank said.

Faith sobbed louder.

"Why are you crying?"

"You have no idea?" She shook her head. "You only think of yourself. I married an asshole." She hissed, taking a step back, proud to stand up for herself.

"Well, that's nice." Frank retorted.

Faith tilted her head. "What? You really have no idea how inconsiderate you are. Truly oblivious." She shook her head. A small part of her felt bad that she had retaliated but she couldn't figure out why since he'd treated her like shit for so long. *Why?* Why did she feel bad about telling him how she felt? Why was it her job to always make sure he was okay, when he never thought a single second about what she needed? *Selfish.* He was proving his selfishness more each day. He had to know that how he was behaving wasn't okay, but deep down, she knew that he didn't understand. She was tired of teaching him year after year how an adult should behave; how she should be treated. But he couldn't be taught. And he didn't make any effort to learn. She had had enough of him; her children were her priority now. Would she have the courage to do it on her own even though she had been doing it on her own all along?

Nurses came in one-by-one. "You have to keep it down. Is everything okay?" Faith was annoyed that she was finally finding her voice, but to the outside world she was considered the problem.

Once she composed herself enough to be able to breathe, the nurses escorted her to the elevator, mostly so she wouldn't change her mind and stay. Even though she desperately needed to get some air, it was hard for her to leave. What if Frank couldn't handle it? What if Kyle stopped breathing, would he know what to do? Would it be easier to just stay with Kyle and allow Frank to frolic at lunch in the real world without a care? She kissed Kyle on the forehead, secretly hoping he'd wake up for Frank to experience all the things; the crying, the reflux, the diapers, the monitors beeping every time he stopped breathing. She wished for him to experience cold, cardboard-like grilled cheese sandwiches with a cup of green Jell-O and a pack of two graham crackers, again. She cried all the way down the hallway, to the parking garage, to the highway. Cars blew past her like meteorites while she struggled to speed up. It was as if she had forgotten how to excel in order to merge. Cars beeped.

Her eyes focused on her exit sign while driving past it; the exit where Jenna was home with the in-laws, where she should have been, cuddling her first born. Thick, sludgy mom guilt formed in her chest and the tears made it hard to see where she was going.

"Girl, you look like you've been put through the ringer." Her hairdresser thought she'd seen all of Faith's emotions over the last decade; wrong boyfriends, job changes, sharing alcoholic incident stories, but this time Faith seemed beyond help and she couldn't find the words to comfort her. "You cannot feel guilty for doing something for yourself." The hairdresser said. "He needs to step up." She knew she was right. Her hairdresser was always right. Despite her exhaustion, Faith made it through the appointment and home, passing out in her own bed until the sun woke her up sixteen hours later; no alarms, no two-hour feeding shifts, no doctors. Maybe the in-laws *had* taken the car to Chili's, she would never have known. Jenna climbed into her bed and they cuddled for the rest of the morning.

On her way back to the hospital, Frank called with a diagnosis. Dual diagnoses to be exact. "Viral Meningitis and diGeorge Syndrome 22 something-something". Her heart began racing. "What does that mean?"

"How am I supposed to know?" He growled.

"You're there, they talked to you. What did they say?"

There was silence on the other end of the line.

"I knew I shouldn't have left."

"Calm down. Supposedly, the Meningitis is a brain infection and has a two-week incubation period. So do you think he picked it up when you brought the kids to the petting zoo a few weeks ago?"

Faith didn't appreciate the insinuation. "I never took him out of the carrier." Faith remembered.

"Hmmm," Frank sighed, condescendingly.

She pulled her car over to the side of the road, cars beeped while she skidded to a stop. "How long will he be in the hospital? Will he be okay?"

"I guess we can bring him home now."

"What are you talking about? That's it? We've been sitting there for a week and that's it?"

"Let me look at my notes." Frank rustled a paper. "They said that since the Meningitis is viral and not bacterial, no meds would help. He will just get better on his own. They're going to keep him one more night just to be sure."

Faith was trying to make sense of it. "What about his oxygen levels? We just take him off the monitors and hope it's okay?"

"Look, I don't know." He interrupted. "When are you coming back so I can go home?"

"Are you kidding me right now?" Her voice got louder. "Never … never," Faith screamed into Frank's ear before hanging up on him. She leaned her head back in the seat before she finished screaming. When she was done she typed in diGeorge Syndrome on her phone and saw words like "disorder" and "missing part of chromosome 22". "22q.11". While she read on, her head spun with the possibilities of Kyle having any of the one hundred and eighty different symptoms. *One hundred and eighty.* Her eyes widened while she read on. "Heart defects, thyroid issues, poor immune system function, cleft palate, calcium issues, delayed development, behavioral problems, emotional problems, facial features, small chin, low-set ears, wide-set eyes or a narrow groove in the upper lip, palate problems, learning disabilities, behavior problems, developmental delays, speech delays, growth delays, failure to thrive, difficulty feeding, failure to gain weight, gastrointestinal problems, breathing problems, poor muscle tone … schizophrenia? …" *The list kept getting worse. Why wasn't this found in utero? Heart defects is a symptom of this syndrome?* Faith wasn't sure she could compose herself in order to get back on the road. She was partly in a rush to be with Kyle, but mostly stalling, not in a rush to relieve Frank who had only been there a fraction of the time that she had.

Faith's phone rang. She recognized the number as

a version of her work number and answered. "Hi," she cleared her throat. "This is Faith … Yes, this is she … What? … Uh huh … Yes I'm still here." Her voice shook but she tried not to let her hear it. "But I'm scheduled to come in next week … after my maternity leave is over … I just talked to my boss the other day about what we'd be doing when I come back. Okay … Yes … I understand." She opened her mouth to respond, but nothing came out. Before she had a chance to process it, her boss called.

"They already called."

"They called you already?" He asked. "What did they say?"

"They said they were letting me go."

"Geez." He sighed. "I told them not to call you before I talked to you."

"You knew about this?"

"Faith, I didn't want this. I was trying to fight for you. To figure out a solution. We were working something out. It's not fair."

"I understand." Faith told him. But the truth was, it was all too overwhelming to even think about. Even though the trucks and cars sped past her, it seemed like slow motion; a nightmare. *Meningitis, brain infection, turning blue, divorce, special needs, doctors, specialists, "syndrome", sick.* Wind from the passing vehicles shook her car. She looked out the window feeling scared and alone. The money she would have earned at work in the next few months would have fully funded the mediator. How could she do that with no job? Could the money she stashed away in her private savings be enough? *Kyle's sick again.* One more ear infection and he would need tubes. The poor child was sick three weeks out of every month since he was born. No daycare would take him with fevers all the time. Frank never took a day off from work to help her. *And now, meningitis?*

Dianna knew something was terribly wrong when Faith called and didn't say anything on the other end. "Hold on, don't hang up, I'm doing something but I can talk … hang on." Dianna took a moment to run to a quiet place to chat privately. "I can't believe it," Dianna said. She was speechless too.

"Kyle will bounce back. Am I sure? No, I'm terrified, but I have to believe it. And now I can't get divorced." Faith blabbered through her tears. "I won't have that kind of money. He won't leave the house and I won't be able to afford something without a job. I'm stuck. I'm stuck with him."

"That sucks."

Faith inhaled. Dianna had always known what to say. She'd always taken her side or at least had always been there to see her point of view. She knew Faith well enough to know that she was taking her comment the wrong way.

"What I mean is, yes, Kyle will be fine. He's in a great hospital and I know you'll do everything you can for him. All that you can do. We certainly know shithead won't."

"Tell me how you really feel." Faith tried to make a joke.

"I mean it's miserable to feel that you're stuck. This isn't the 1950's anymore. I often wonder how our lives would have been if our parents and grandparents had gone their separate ways.

"It might have been better off for everyone." Faith admitted. "But I can't do this with no job."

"I thought you were saving up to make the move."

"I was. But now…"

"You still can."

Dianna was always so positive, even if a bit unrealistic, a free spirit. Everything would work out. Faith had to trust.

Everyone was happy when Kyle was sent home to recover. No buzzing monitors and doctors at all hours made for a smoother recovery. Being that she now thought she could not get divorced, because of money, she decided to stay without telling Frank any definite plans. She figured if she could simply ignore him, then life in the same house could be tolerated. Over the next few weeks whenever he entered a room she was in, she left. She waited and never entered a room he was in if she could help it. It didn't take long before he started to figure it out, following her from room to room.

"Whenever I come into the room, you leave."

"Whenever you come into the room, you badger me."

"I want to talk."

"I have nothing more to say." And it was true. She had no more words, and no more empathy. He wasn't going to change. Their life would always be the same.

"I don't know how much more of this I can take," she

told Dianna on the phone while she reached out onto the porch to get the mail. "He's driving me up a wall."

"First of all, are you safe?"

"Yeah, it's nothing like that."

"Okay. But for what it's worth, for better or for worse doesn't mean someone's *allowed* to make your life miserable. Call around for apartments; you never know if you don't start looking. You might have enough saved."

Faith ripped open an envelope from work. "Oh my God, Dianna."

"What, what?" Dianna waited.

"The severance check. The amount."

"Girl, use your words, what are you talking about?"

"My severance check," Faith tried to catch her breath and looked up to the sky, clasping the paper to her chest. "It's almost to the penny of what the mediator estimated it would cost."

"It's a sign." They said in unison.

Faith threw herself into the next chapter of her life between tears, doubt, and strength from somewhere. The next several months of the mediation process became a complete mess. Frank tried to drag it out in order for her to run out of the little money he thought she had. Every penny, every asset, every belonging was fought over. Whose was it? Who bought it? Who brought it to the marriage? They couldn't discuss anything without an argument. The tension between them was so palpable they had to take separate cars to the mediator's office. The anxiety of having to be anywhere alone with him only to be berated made her neck break out in stress hives.

Throughout mediation and mandatory parenting classes, Frank said things like, "Well, you want this divorce, not me. The kids are better off with both parents. I still love you." Week after week his words became meaningless. His continued actions didn't prove that he had any intention of making things better, for her, their family, or himself. She was done with him, with the marriage, with his antics so his words no longer had any power over her. She had no more tears left to cry. As the months of mediation continued forward, the relationship that was once defined by love, was now manufactured into a business transaction, slogging on toward the iceberg.

If he had any power over her at all, it was that he didn't want her to tell anyone until his parents knew. And he wasn't going to tell them over the phone. It had to be in person. Her person. That made for a fun trip to visit them for their pre-scheduled yearly trip that they hadn't cancelled. Faith had considered not going with them. Frank would never be able to handle both kids in an airport alone. *What if Jenna had to go to the bathroom? What if Frank did?* Faith decided that Frank needed her help and plus, she desperately needed a vacation. There was no way he would be going without her. She looked forward to soaking up some Florida sunshine, maybe even reading a whole book.

-11-

People whispered not so quiet comments about having to share a plane with potentially noisy children. Faith wasn't that thrilled either. She'd always been one to wonder why people didn't leave their children home when they traveled or why the parents didn't reprimand them when they cried. But, alas, that was before children. And, as it turned out, leaving them home wasn't an option, and you cannot always control a screaming baby. Go figure.

Frank balanced Kyle on his lap and leaned over Jenna toward Faith's seat on the plane. "We can't tell my parents about the divorce," he whispered.

It was the first time she heard him say the word. "Frank, that's the whole point of going down to Florida together. Because you didn't want to tell them on the phone." She twisted the ring on her left hand, not believing what was happening. "What are we going to do, spring it on them after it's final? We have to tell them."

"No," he stood firm. The flight attendant leaned in to ask if Jenna wanted a coloring book, happy to break any tension that was happening with a cheerful "yes!"

Faith zoned out on the plane, staring at the seat in front of her, transported to her wedding day.

They were about to cut the cake and Frank was starting to get buzzed. He put his beer down by the cake, a seemingly innocent gesture, but Faith did NOT want the bottle in the photos, time stamped in perpetuity. When she asked him to move it, it became a thing. Why did she have to explain? People were gathering around them waiting for happy cake photos. She knew the bottle wasn't moved far enough out of the shot. The DJ instructed her through the speakers to grab the knife and start the first cut. The photographer told Frank to put his hand over hers for the photo and look up. The music blared. Everyone waited. Frank criticized Faith that she wasn't cutting the cake right. She stopped to look at him, trying to tell him to stop through gritted teeth. People still waited. The photographer told them to look up and smile. "Pretend you love each other," she said. The world began spinning. His behavior. The beer bottle. The loud music. Pretend you love each other. "It's okay," she thought, "it's not like I have to marry him." Terror washed over her face and she looked out into the sea of camera flashes and cheers, "... oh shit I already did." Snap. That photo; Faith's deer in the headlight reaction, the angry crease in Frank's forehead, his mouth open telling her what she was doing wrong, the beer bottle tucked behind the cake but still in view was the beginning of the end. Her sign; the bricks thrown at her head that she didn't listen to. She always came back for more. The room spun around her. She heard a gasp and the room went dark. She woke up on the floor in a puddle of tulle and lace. Frank was at the bar

being "comforted".

"Mama, look at my drawing." Jenna beamed. Faith leaned over the plane's armrest and kissed her on the top of her sweet head.

"Yes, baby. That's beautiful." She swallowed hard. *Our family.*

"Drinks?" The flight attendant interrupted.

Frank toggled back and forth from the flight attendant to Faith, debating on ordering something other than a soda.

"Seriously?" Faith wasn't surprised anymore.

"What?"

"This isn't a joke anymore. This is serious."

"I know it's serious."

"I don't think you do. I'm telling them."

After settling everyone in to the in-law's house, and taking a tour of the former guest room, now 'Mini's' new art studio, Faith helped with the salad and lunch settings. She guessed by looking at Mini that they didn't eat much salad anymore, or ever.

"Grandma–"

"It's 'Mini' honey," Mini interrupted. "I'm too young to be called "Grandma".

"Mini … why you Mini not 'Biggie'?" Jenna asked.

Grampy almost spit out his drink. Honest Jenna looked up waiting for an answer.

"Honey, Mini already explained her nickname," Faith said, trying not to smirk. "Now, drink your milk and eat your lunch so you can swim in the pool. Mommy and Daddy have something to talk to your grandparents about." Frank's eyes widened. The landline phone rang and Grampy ran to answer it before they hung up.

"What? What is it?" Mini tried to motion to Grampy for some clues.

"Kelly's in the hospital. She had some sort of hallucinations and they found out the brain tumor's back."

"Kelly who?" Mini asked.

"Kelly, your daughter-in-law." Grampy whispered, covering the phone.

"Auntie Kelly?" Jenna asked.

"You're very smart, Jenna. Yes, Auntie Kelly." Mini said.

"Is she okay?" Faith asked.

Grampy waved at everyone to be quiet. "She'll be fine. She will have to have the tumor removed again. Right now it seems to be the same as last time. Just a long recovery process," he said, covering the phone.

"We're definitely not telling them now." Frank warned.

"Should we cancel going to the park tomorrow?" Faith asked Mini.

"No, there's nothing we can do from here. They'll keep in touch if they need us. Let's bring the kids to the park tomorrow," Mini planned. Faith was looking forward to getting out of the house with something else to do.

The entrance to the park was inundated by people when Mini, Grampy, and Faith's family showed up; strollers, diaper bags and all. Frank rushed ahead to the front of the line and tried to sneak in between two families, fully expecting all of them to follow suit. He waved them in but they stayed behind. He was practically plastered against the back of a man's sweaty t-shirt. They could see the man inching up for space until he had no more space and turned around to confront him. "Don't worry about it," Frank said, as if it was his right to cut the entire line. A stress rash formed on Faith's chest and radiated up her neck into her cheeks.

"What is he doing?" Mini asked.

"The usual." Faith shrugged.

"What is his problem?" Mini asked.

"Exactly." Faith replied. "Happy, happy, we're on vacation," Faith sing-songed. "Happiest place on earth."

They spent the next few days getting updates on Kelly's brain tumor or simply ignoring Frank's behavior. Faith tried to recuperate from the stress that had accumulated over the last year but it was difficult with him there. She tried to read a book on the lanai while Kyle was napping when Frank sauntered by whispering "big ass belly" loud enough for her to hear.

"Can you cut it out and leave me alone?"

"When are you going to cool down? You still have a hair across your ass."

"I wonder why," she said, throwing her hands up. She saw Mini in the corner of her eye coming toward her mid-hand gesture. Faith's eyes widened and she faked a smile.

"Faith," Mini sounded like Faith was about to be scolded for speaking to her son in such a way. "Why don't you get lost for a while," she suggested and gave her directions to the nearest shopping plaza. It was the first time in a long time that she would be able to relax. Faith took her time browsing, shopping and even enjoyed an extra large ice cream, sundae-style, leaving no evidence behind. She dawdled back a few hours later.

"When we told you to 'get lost for a while' you really did." Mini joked.

"I never have a break, Mini. Frank does nothing. Ever. Besides it took an hour and a half to get there and ba–"

Faith heard Frank's words bellowing from the lanai, a place that used to be her favorite. She'd always planned to retire and own a similar shady, cool place, screened in from the bugs and the crawly clingy things, with a crystal clear pool overlooking water. It was the perfect place to read or write or paint. She stopped mid-sentence when she heard Frank's words. Slow. Drawn out. "Are you kidding me?"

Mini laughed. "The boys went out for a few drinks while you were gone."

"A few drinks? Mini, he can't have a few drinks," she started toward the lanai, "he's an alcoholic."

"Don't you think you're exaggerating?" Mini said.

"This …" Faith stuttered. "This is why he doesn't think he has a problem … This is why we're…" Faith stopped. It wasn't her place to tell her about the divorce. She was so used to trying to keep the peace and Frank specifically told her not to say anything. The divorce was all her fault, Frank was sure to remind her. If his drinking was such a problem, she imagined them saying, then why did she stick around so long? He'd only had one beer. Oh my God, her eyes opened wide. One beer was never one. One equals six. And six equals a 12-pack and waking up in a puddle of urine. Oh, how Mini would love that in her guest bed. Not only was Frank hanging off the wagon, it was going to run him over too. "Poor little Faith" … nagging him again about having one beer …

"Grampy's no angel either," Mini interrupted, throwing her head back to laugh boisterously. "They'll never change." She said it so matter-of-factly that Faith wondered if she registered it right; but she did. It haunted her for the rest of the trip. *They'll never change. They'll never change.* It was the slightest glimpse into the rollercoaster ride she'd already endured, that literally would never end if she stayed with him; the selfish man-child who idolized his parents. The man couldn't make a single decision without asking his mother even though he should have been talking to Faith. He couldn't do anything without running ideas past his parents, personal family matters, children's health issues, he did everything they said and nothing that they didn't. He didn't even wear his wedding ring because his father didn't, for different reasons entirely, keeping his ring in the cup holder of the car in case he got pulled over so he'd look more 'responsible'.

He was out drinking with his father because they told him it would be okay. He could have just one. He was on vacation. And didn't have a problem. Leaving her home alone while he flirted with skanks at the strip club was a way of letting off steam because he worked so hard day in and day out as an accountant.

Faith looked up, speechless. *He thinks it's okay. Jenna will too. What am I teaching my daughter?* Mini's matter-of-fact phrase was the insight into the next thirty years with Frank and she wanted out. Faith felt sick to her stomach. Frank and his family's behavior was the permission Faith needed to know that she was making the right choice. *Nothing would change if I stay. Nothing would change.*

It was a long rest of the trip, but Frank's badgering at every opportunity began having less effect on her, swarming around her like a gnat now that she had a clearer vision of what to do. Her choice was made. She would leave it to Frank to tell them. When? She didn't care. It was all him now.

Back home in her comfortable kitchen she tended to the children and counted the minutes for Frank to leave the house in order to breathe a sigh of relief. The stress aura that surrounded him left with him, every time. She wished she could stay in her adorable little cape; eleven hundred square feet, three bedrooms, one bath with a postage stamp size lot and old-fashioned shutters framing the windows. It was perfect for her and the two kids. But alas, Frank had already told her that he'd never allow her to stay in the house without him. And one thing was sure, he never expected she would have enough money and actually move out. She inhaled for strength to make the call.

"And your work number," the man on the other line asked.

"No," she hedged.

"And your work number," he repeated.

"Nope," Faith didn't want him to ask again. Eventually she explained her situation. "Yes, yes, I can meet you there in one hour." She thanked him profusely.

While the landlord unlocked the door Faith looked out the window in the small stairway to see that the yard below was fully fenced in. Cheerful warm sunlight spilled in from every window. She could breathe there, already. The hardwoods, knicked and weathered, welcomed her the way her grandparents' old home did. She could practically picture homemade soup on the stove and hear the history of the house in the creaks of the floorboards. The rooms led in a circle, living room, dining room, bedrooms, to the kitchen and around. Jenna would love running from room to room like Faith had when she was a child, she imagined. Etched tin panels on the ceiling in the kitchen and the large pantry reminded her of her grandparent's house. The yellow cookie jar hidden in plain view on the top shelf taunted her. She would sneak in there when no one was looking.

The dining room would be her office, and the living room would double as her bedroom, she decided. The kids would have their own rooms especially since Kyle stayed up most of the night. She could get to him quickly that way. The laundry hook up was in the kitchen and the dryer was in the pantry, so she never needed to run down to the basement, which was plenty large enough to store all of her bins from the house. "I love it. I'll take it."

"Great! I will need a credit check, first month, last month and security deposit, plus a co-signer. Meet me at my office at six-thirty and call me if anything changes." He handed her his business card.

The last thing Faith wanted was to ask her mother for anything. She knew her parents didn't have the money in case she defaulted on payment, but she knew that her savings would hold her over for at least one year. It would be the only way for him to accept her application. Surely she'd find a job within a year and have nothing holding her back. She thought.

Her parents met her at the landlord's office. Fortunately, or not, he was a lawyer also. He combed over his excessively long rental agreement and numerous stipulations in legal speak which included not getting her security deposit back if there was damage to the apartment. His list went on for several minutes and pages.

"I don't know," her mother chimed in, looking at her portion to read and sign.

"Babs…" her father started.

Her mother interrupted. "I don't like this, I'm not signing this," pushing the papers away. "I'm going to put the kibosh on this whole thing."

Faith gasped. "Mom … you saw the apartment and liked it. You knew I needed you to co-sign, why do you think you're here? Please," Faith whispered. "I need to get out. I'm *dying* living in the house with him, how do you not see this?"

"Don't worry about it." Her mother said.

Faith froze. "Mom, please. I won't be late on the rent. I have money saved up."

Silence filled the room.

The landlord excused himself to let them discuss, but they could still see his shadow in front of the door.

"I don't want to be on the hook if she doesn't pay the

rent."

"Babs, she'll be fine. She'll find a job."

"What if she doesn't?"

"Well, she can't stay where she is." Her father grabbed the pen.

Faith signed the final signature with a heaviness in her heart for that which she'd lost; her home, her marriage and the maternal compassion and closeness from her mother that she still craved.

-12-

Faith wasted no time packing up the house with her many bins of pre-relationship belongings that she would bring to her new apartment, leaving items for Frank that she thought would be fair, including any baggage that sparked ill feelings. Every night when Frank came home, more grocery store banana boxes, crates and bins were stacked with her stuff.

Moving day and her first night sleeping in her new apartment arrived a week later. Faith didn't have the raw emotions of regret she'd expected when she woke up, even if she was sleeping on an air mattress, waiting for her furniture, it was better than spending one more night in the house with Frank. Instead, she was accepting a hot cup of tea from Dianna at her new doorstep, excited. That is until Frank and his brothers showed up at her new place to help. Frank remained in the distance, observing.

"I know you're divorcing our brother, but you're still family. Call us anytime you need anything." They said.

Faith nodded and hugged them goodbye when they were done.

Frank watched and walked toward her, strangely calm and not shaky. "I understand why you needed to do this."

Faith stepped back, "Do you?"

He squinted at her. "I want to see the kids though."

"Only if you're sober." Her eyes widened, waiting for an answer.

"Hmmm." His forehead creased and his left eyelid twitched. He tried to cover it with one hand.

"I hope you *are* able to do this for their sakes, *and yours*." She paused and looked at him; really looked at him for the first time in several months. She hadn't stood near him in quite some time and surprised herself when a twinge of pity flickered within her.

"I still love you." Frank said.

"I …" Faith struggled. She could hear Dianna choking in the distance. "I ... don't ... *anymore*." Faith could barely get the words out.

Dianna ran over, out of breath, hooking her arm in Faith's, whirling her around and away from Frank. "Show me where this cute new cookie jar goes." They headed toward the door. "What the hell was that?" Dianna whispered.

"I just … I feel sorry for him."

"That's because he's sober, maybe, for this second."

"True." Faith sighed.

"What?" Dianna demanded.

"No, I'm good. Really." Faith said. "I was just thinking … even if he has changed, I don't want him … anymore. I'm happier now."

"This is only the beginning Faith. I want my old friend back. But for now, I see a glimpse of her. Smart, strong, decisive."

They walked into the house, leaving Frank standing in the driveway. He yelled after her. "The kids will know this is all you. That this is *your* decision to leave."

Faith's eyes widened.

"And there it is." Dianna said, shaking her head, shoving Faith inside her new stress-free, sunny home.

"I'll see you at the courthouse tomorrow." He continued.

"Gladly," Dianna yelled, flipping him off before shutting the door.

-13-

Faith arrived early to the courthouse on the day of their divorce in order to remain as calm and collected as she'd been when she woke up. Plus, she didn't want to be badgered by Frank alone in the elevator, trying to tell her she was making a mistake. Divorce court wasn't the way she'd learned it would be from television. Instead, it was a quick shuffling in and out of people. Everyone heard each other's business while they waited for their turn to be called from their seats to the judge's bench. And even the tallest person still had to look up, appearing timid. They watched the judge being empathetic in certain cases, almost soft. Sometimes His Honor threw the book at a deadbeat and wouldn't even let him talk. Faith's stomach turned in queasy anticipation.

When it was her turn, it went smoothly. Many months of mediation had prepared her for this moment. Each and every item was fought over, picked through and divvied up; their entire marriage reduced to a business transaction. But Faith was ready. There was nothing left to fight over.

"Are you ready?" The mediator asked before they left her office for the last time.

Faith recalled having to take two cars to the mediator's office only then to be badgered by Frank in the waiting area. Most times, Faith would sit in the car and enter exactly on time or a minute late so she wouldn't have to talk to him directly.

"Yes." Faith and Frank both said.

"I know you are." The mediator said, looking directly at Faith.

The mediator had prepared everything ahead of time and they were out of the courtroom in no time at all. Faith's voice was stronger than when she had spoken aloud at all the previous formal appearances over the last several months; the times she had to plead her stance on custody, family court, ending the marriage, even the marriage counselor. She remained unfazed when rehashing their relationship, unresolved problems, listing the reasons she had for divorce, where the children would go, would she change her name back to her maiden name? "Yes, Your Honor, I'm sure." She locked eyes with him and nodded. The judge looked at her over his black-rimmed reading glasses and nodded back.

Faith practically high-fived her mediator and gave her a huge hug when the judge hit the gavel. A tremendous sense of relief washed over her and her smile spanned miles. *I did it!* While celebrating silently, she caught sight of Frank watching her in the hallway. Completely caught off-guard by his tears, she inhaled all the strength of the thousand times he had slammed the door in her face and left her crying. She turned on her heel and walked in the other direction; toward freedom, toward peace, toward healing.

She walked faster through the building and outside to

the parking garage, pulling out her phone to dial Dianna. But before she lifted the phone to her ear, Frank appeared. She looked around for security or any other person, but the parking garage was desolate.

"So…" Frank cleared his throat. "This is a break, not a break up, right?"

Faith nearly choked. "Are you serious, Frank? You wouldn't give me the satisfaction of a separation, you wouldn't leave the house, you made me uproot my life, my kids, find a two-bedroom apartment; I'm sleeping on a couch. Even with all of this looming," she pointed all around, "you still didn't take it seriously. You still chose alcohol over your family and didn't get help. I hope you do get help, Frank. I do. But we are divorced. It's final. Don't you get that?" She thought he was going to apologize or kiss her. She stepped back.

"You'll come back."

She laughed, shaking her head. "Not a chance." She got in her car and locked the door, backing out, leaving him standing in the parking garage watching her leave.

-14-

Faith gathered her children in each arm and snuggled them on the couch in her new apartment. She closed her eyes and breathed in their skin, their hair, covering them with the hugs and kisses she so desperately needed. Warm sunlight poured in through the windows and she inhaled without the weight of an elephant sitting on her chest.

The following day she had prepared for Kyle's ear tube surgery. Frank had already informed her that he wouldn't attend the surgery. Faith was relieved that she wouldn't have to endure passing time with him in the waiting room and knew she could do it on her own. It would be one of the quickest and easiest surgeries on the long list of issues that could happen to Kyle in his lifetime. She would plan to force Frank to be at a more important surgery in the future perhaps. But being at this surgery would be less stressful alone, she hoped. She clenched her fists for extra assurance.

She packed everything for both kids and herself, even an overnight bag in case something went wrong at the hospital with anesthesia, or during Kyle's surgery because of his small airways. She was prepared. Plus, her grand-mother's superstitious tendencies crept in so if she hadn't prepared for a hospital overnight, she'd surely have to stay. It was left over from the five-day viral meningitis fiasco that she wasn't prepared for.

Anything with 22q was possible. What she wasn't prepared for was being turned away at check-in and sent home because Kyle spiked a fever and was too congested from the ear infection to perform the surgery. The point of the surgery was to clear his ears, his chronic congestion and infections. In the end, the day was a bust. The surgical team and anesthesiologists deemed his procedure unsafe. All the planning. All the nerves. They'd have to repeat medicines and the process after another round of antibiotics.

-15-

In the meantime, Faith supervised Frank's visitations until she couldn't stand being badgered and followed around in her own home. "Frank, this time is supposed to be spent playing with them, not following me around telling me this is all my fault. Go. Be with them." She dumped a load of laundry to be washed.

"You need to find a job," Frank cornered her.

"I'm trying." Faith admitted. "Look, I'm done here. I'm going out."

"Where?"

"Out. You … spend time with the kids. That's why you're here. Leave me alone." She went to Jenna's room where she was playing alone, kissed her and whispered to her. "Have fun with Daddy, I'm going to go get some stuff at the store. Back in a little while." Faith rushed out and drove around the corner to the nearest grocery store. She checked her email quickly before getting out. She'd been sending out dozens of resumes and job applications to no avail. Once composed, she took her time down the aisles, stalling, enjoying a bit of peace with no children in tow.

Frank didn't believe her and filed an appeal to force

Faith to report each job she'd applied for per week. Some jobs he thought he had a right to disapprove of, like cashier, but she was trying, finally accepting a temp job. Although it wasn't ideal, she would be filling in for a Director who was going on maternity leave and Faith hoped it would turn into more opportunities at the end of the contract. It was a similar corporate environment to the one she'd been used to working in. She'd prove herself. Like before. Faith hurried to try on her old pantsuits, button jackets, and heels, bouncing down the hallway with excitement and a paycheck on the horizon.

What should have taken twenty-minutes took her an hour and ten minutes in rush hour traffic, one way. That meant that she would be away from the kids ten plus hours a week just to sit in traffic. But she would be working again.

"I'm not paying for a babysitter."

"Frank, you've been pestering me to find a job. How else am I supposed to work? They're not in school yet, what do you want me to do with them? Are you going to help?"

"I work."

"I am too, now. Which means you'll have to take fifty percent of the doctor's visits."

Frank hadn't considered her value of being a stay-at-home mom when he pushed the work issue. He only wished for his child support to be reduced.

After a few weeks of dropping the kids off to the nicest in-home babysitter ever, the commute started to wear on her. She was sure to give the finger to the same fifty-five mile per hour speed limit sign every day while she crawled past it; a new-found gesture she'd learned in her independence. But the commute that used to signify a salary, savings, nest egg, goals … now signified the second floor of a hundred year old home with drafty windows, no dishwasher and on street parking during the worst snowstorms to hit New England in decades. No longer did she park her car in her garage. Instead she was shoveling her car out, moving it on odd numbered days and carrying groceries and baby car seats up stairs. Still, whenever she turned that key to her own place, the stress washed away immediately. A paycheck would be coming soon and that helped.

Faith enjoyed getting out of the house, putting on work clothes and makeup. She didn't have to worry about Jenna and Kyle because they were at an awesome daycare where they were loved and happy. Until the third time the babysitter called in three weeks. Kyle had a fever, again. With his compromised immune system and other children in close proximity, it was only a matter of time. It had to be his ears, again.

"Frank, you need to pick up Kyle at the sitter, he's sick."

"I'm working."

"Seriously? I just started this job. And it's temporary. I cannot take another day off."

"Neither can I."

"Frank, I'm not asking. I'm telling you to help me so I can keep my job."

"I have to work and keep my job. It's more important."

"It's always about you Frank. Even when we were married, you didn't help." Faith hung up the phone and left work to pick up Kyle. The pediatrician confirmed that Kyle had another ear infection. They couldn't get a handle on his healthy days to fix his problem. Kyle would need to be out of daycare for twenty-four hours until his fever cleared.

"I understand." Faith told her new company when she told them that she couldn't come back to work the next day, again. They told her in no uncertain terms this time, to not bother coming back.

She pushed her fingers deep into her temples and looked over at Kyle cuddled up, trying to breathe with red cheeks and a stuffy nose. "How? How am I supposed to work when you're so sick all the time?" She scooped him up and rested her cheek on his warm face.

"What's wrong mama?" Jenna said.

"Nothing honey. Go get a game and we'll play."

"OK," she bounced away, coming back with a puzzle, absolutely sure not to wake her brother so she could have the Mommy-and-me time she craved since Faith had tried to go back to work. Faith needed it too.

By the time the surgery day arrived and Faith brought Kyle home from the hospital, she was barely able to form her words from sheer exhaustion. She needed a break and Frank was the only person she could call to help. She couldn't burden Dianna and her parents weren't comfortable caring for such a medically complex child who *still* refluxed every feeding out of his nose. It was all Faith's responsibility all the time. She prayed that Frank would step up.

Faith's eyes darted toward the front door when she heard the stairs creak. Jenna opened it for Frank before his hand knocked for their first visitation overnight. "Daddy." Her words sounded more pronounced. She wanted to keep the kids at her house, especially after Kyle's surgery to keep an eye on him, but she was desperate for a break and some adult interaction. Her mind flip-flopped between wanting to go out to wanting to stay home. Plus, she had decided that she wanted to sing again and because she made the commitment with Dianna's urging, she was obligated to go. She still had that Catholic guilt of not cancelling plans especially for church even though she was no longer a Catholic. Decades of speeches about not wasting talents and being of service to others, flooded back. Besides, choir practice would be over early and she could be in bed by 8:15 if she needed to.

She inspected Frank for any signs of alcohol. She stood as close to him as possible, circling him like a wolf, focusing in, inspecting.

"What are you doing?" he asked.

"Have you been drinking?"

"No. I was at work." He grabbed the middle of his neck tie and shook it in her face.

Faith rolled her eyes. "And you won't drink tonight while they're at your house?"

"Nope. I quit." He said, pleased with himself.

Faith side-eyed him, shaking a brown paper bag of medicines for Frank to give Kyle with clear instructions. She wanted to believe him. She thought twice to let Frank have the kids overnight, that night especially, but he said he could handle it.

Faith tasted blood, having bitten her lip the whole way to the church. Doing something new, starting with the choir, meeting new people, doing something for herself seemed like a good idea days ago. She pushed her new anxiety down.

She stood inside the vestibule, admiring the simplicity of the bare wooden cross above the altar in contrast to the gaudy décor of the Catholic Church where she'd grown up. She'd researched and found this congregation when she found out that Frank wasn't allowed to marry her in the Catholic Church because of an unresolved issue with his previous marriage. She remembered walking down the aisle slowly, taking the time to smile at family and friends who were there to support her. It wasn't until she approached the very end of the aisle that she realized it was Frank who was waiting for her at the altar; she inhaled sharply. Her heart started to beat faster. She'd been so caught up in the minutia of the wedding; plans, making handmade invitations, finding the fluffiest gown her mother wanted. She'd dreamed of it since she was a child, wearing her father's white undershirts on her head like a cascading veil, running around like a princess. The pastor greeted her. Last week he had told her to get over her hesitation and that it was just cold feet. She was getting married! To Frank!

One of the choir ladies startled her when she linked arms with her and ushered her in to the front to meet the other choir members. Faith tried not to breathe in the scent of her shower body powder. "I'm glad you came.

It's so good to see you." She patted her hand with her cold gnarled fingers. Faith sat for vocal warm-ups and scrunched her nose wondering which one's sweater smelled like mothballs. Her phone echoed loudly in her music bag and she apologized profusely while she fumbled to fish it out. Frank's name flashed on the display.

"I'm busy," she whispered. "Is everything okay?"

"So…" Frank interrupted. "Ah…" He proceeded nervously. Faith was used to his anxiety and pictured him pacing and rubbing his face. She rolled her eyes and excused herself, walking quickly to the back of the church. "I see the pink medicine," he said, "and put it in his ears, but I just noticed this little bottle, what is this for?"

Faith paused. "You did what?"

"I put the pink drops in his ears."

"Are you serious? That's Tylenol." She tried to keep her voice down while her heart raced.

"What's the little bottle?"

Her eyes widened trying to process his question. "That's the ear drops. I knew you were incapable. I CAN NOT believe this." She threw her hands up, her voice getting louder. "That Tylenol will goop up in there and crystalize. What were you thinking? I knew this wasn't a good idea. I knew it." She paced. There was no answer. "Is he in pain?"

"I don't think so."

"What should I do?"

"Call the freakin' doctor." She looked up at the cross at the front of the church and apologized to the heavens. "You should have called him already." She hung up and dialed the doctor on call who tried to make her feel better by saying he'd seen it before. She knew he hadn't. Kyle would be fine and Faith called Frank back, but it depleted any confidence in him that she may have had to begin with. By the time she called Frank back, he still hadn't called the doctor.

Ruining her one night out in ages, she left early after apologizing and called Dianna on the way home.

"What can you do? You can't do anything about it at home and you can't go to Frank's. He needs to step up and be a dad and take care of it. Kyle will be fine."

Faith remained silent.

"Meet me at Joe's Restaurant," Dianna said.

"I'm tired."

"You're always tired. Look, you're dressed aren't you?"

Faith sighed.

"I'm just getting off my shift. Come out with me. You'll still be in bed by nine."

"Good point." Faith agreed, pulling off at the next exit instead of going home.

"Is Joe here?" Faith asked.

"Somewhere."

"Can you let him know Faith's here?"

"I'll tell him." The bartender threw a beer towel over his shoulder and walked away. Faith knew he wouldn't care to remember. She ran her hand along the bartop, feeling the cool smoothness of the cherry wood and the detail of the engraved filigree. *Joe did a great job with this place.* It was his true love. He spoke about owning a bar since they were kids. It reminded him of visiting his grandfather at the bar he owned in 1970's Brooklyn.

Faith hated sitting on the barstools because her legs dangled, but so what, she wasn't trying to impress anyone. The last time she sat at the bar was the night Frank was trying to impress her, she remembered while waiting for Dianna.

"Hi. I'm Frank." He introduced himself.

"Faith. Nice to meet you." She replied. Faith was caught off guard that he didn't try a dumb pick-up line on her, he simply said hi and Faith had been waiting ages for a real person who didn't play games. Frank paid one hundred percent attention to Faith, didn't check out other girls the way men usually did when they were talking to her, seeing if there were any better choices in the near vicinity. He was shy, awkward, an accountant, stable, she deduced. They spoke closely, using the loud music as an excuse.

Frank kept sneaking kisses on her cheek, and Faith thought it was endearing. She sipped one drink most of the night, he had a few too many. "I don't usually drink this much. You make me nervous," he admitted.

Faith accepted his reasoning without question.

When she slipped off the barstool to use the restroom and he looked down and saw her real height, he made a comment that she was the most adorable thing he had ever seen and Faith was relieved that he wasn't disappointed that she was too short.

He tried to follow her to the bathroom, but she insisted it wasn't necessary. While in line she saw her high school crush.

"Dean." All breath left her body.

"You look great, Faith." Dean said.

Faith blushed.

"You know, I blew it by not dating you. What do you say we give it another shot?" Faith heard Joe wheeze as he walked by. Her jaw dropped but she couldn't form a word. Joe threw his nose in the air like the queen he wanted to be, sauntering away, wagging his finger in the air, swaying his hips.

Faith was inexperienced when she tried to date Dean and he moved quicker than she was ready for. He didn't stick around to teach her any of the essential things in a sexual relationship, things she longed to learn with him since she was completely head-over-heels for him. She would have done anything for him if he'd had the patience. So for him to be standing here with her now, her second chance, every part of her body wanted to say yes. Yes to go home with him and show him everything she'd learned. She wanted to sit in the arena and watch him play hockey again, to be a hockey mom and watch their little players on the ice, to look in his irresistible blue eyes and run her fingers through his sexy blonde hair, but no. No. She was with Frank tonight and made it clear under no uncertain terms that Dean had missed his chance.

Frank interrupted.

Dean looked him over. "Is this creep bothering you?"

"No, he's harmless." Faith told him.

Dean continued, "Faith, please. He's nothing. He's a drunk."

"He just had a little too much to drink. He's fine."

"Think about what I said. You're the one who got away."

"I'm sorry," Faith said. A quick smile formed on her lips. She knew this wouldn't affect him as much as their

breakup hurt her, but knowing there was a little sting was payback enough.

She threw herself into a relationship with Frank and moved in with him after six short months. He must have binge drank on the nights he didn't see her, because she didn't know he had a problem.

"Where were you?" She questioned Frank.

"I had to work late."

"At the bar?"

"You were at art class or choir or something. I didn't know what else to do."

"You didn't know what else to do? Frank, you're not a kid anymore. College drinking days are far behind you. You've got to stop this nonsense. Have one or two and stop after that. I don't understand. Get a hobby. Do something."

"I can stop on my own."

"So do it. Look at you. You're going to ruin your liver, you're going to ruin us."

A group of college kids barreled by bringing Faith back to reality. She realized how sad she must have looked when Dianna snuck up on her and startled her.

Dianna and Faith tried to talk but the music grew louder by the minute. Lights flashed and the band was setting up for the evening. Men of all ages circled around them but Faith wasn't having any of it. It had been years since she'd been anywhere near the dating scene. The pick up lines remained the same though and made them want to laugh out loud. "Those jeans look great on you." Dianna teased. "You know what would look better? If they were on the floor of my apartment… Did it hurt?

When you fell from heaven?"

They moved to a booth to get food and refills.

"You made the right move divorcing him you know?" Dianna said.

"I know. But it's hard."

Dianna puffed her lip. "But look at how good you're doing. You're out of the house. Having an adult beverage."

"I'm tired."

"You're always going to be tired, you have no help. One day that will change. Maybe when you meet husband number two."

"Oh please. Never."

"Never say never. Look at me!" She raised her glass to clink against Faith's. "Incoming, to your right." Faith shifted in her seat at the approaching figure. Dianna giggled.

"I could be his mother." Faith whispered.

"Just have fun," Dianna said.

Faith glanced at her phone. No text from Frank. Surely the kids were settled in bed for the night.

-16-

The chill of New England autumn blew in, frosting the leaves and changing their colors. Crisp apple pie and pumpkin scents reminded her of the perfect family photo taken a long year ago when she thought everything was going to be okay. When she thought Frank was going to stay sober. And the world came crashing down, but Faith kept going.

Birth-to-three added speech therapy even though Kyle wasn't speaking. Still. They all hoped that once his ear tubes went in, that he'd start babbling or responding whenever his name was called, but nothing. The therapists had resorted to depriving him of a toy he wanted in order for him to scream out words but it just made him madder.

Autumn became winter. Winter became spring. The hot kind that felt like Mother Nature forgot spring all together and went straight to summer. Faith was learning how to love life. She spread out her sketchpad and art supplies on a large blanket in their enclosed yard. With Kyle not walking and not crawling but kind of scooting around, he was perfectly happy to be lining up blocks repetitively by her side. The low hum he'd developed to self-soothe was constant. He even hummed while he was eating. Faith always knew where he was. She doodled and sketched ideas and thoughts, enjoying the birds rustling in the trees and the warm sunshine on her skin. Jenna ran in and out of the kiddie pool with grassy feet, bubbles, drippy popsicles and laughter; all the things that made up their perfectly needed respite.

Their bedtime was Faith's time to job hunt, regroup, meditate, draw or simply go to sleep. She took her body's lead on whatever it told her she needed. Many nights she fished her art pad out from between the couch cushions and started sketching motivational quotes and inspirational sayings to gain strength to get herself through the day. "Keep Going." She drew in swirls.

"What'cha doin'?" Dianna asked when Faith answered the phone.

"I'm doodling."

"Fun."

"Don't patronize me."

"Trust me, I'm not. I get that you need to do whatever you need to do to regain your sanity from your life. Those little monsters are twenty-four-seven, talk about stress, money issues, an ex who's…" She didn't finish her thought. "Come out with me tonight."

"I can't."

"I'll pay."

"It's not that. The kids are here tonight."

"He couldn't stay sober for his visitation?"

"That's tomorrow."

"I can't keep it all straight."

"I'm tired anyway."

"You're always tired. Honestly, I think you're depressed."

"I don't think so. I think I was so deep in the bullshit, I lost myself and didn't even realize it."

Dianna agreed.

"And honestly, I'm less lonely now than when I was married to him."

"Wow. That's a pretty big statement."

Faith thought about it and clamped down on the inside of her lip.

"What else is going on?" Dianna asked.

"Well … Jenna is convinced there's a moose in her bedroom."

"Kids are so weird."

"You know you want them."

"Sort of, but you know, if it happens, it happens. So what did you tell her?"

"I made a joke out of it and tickled her and asked her how she thought a moose could possibly walk up the back steps and into her room and she laughed. I thought we were done but then she proceeded to tell me there's a ghost in her room."

"Oh boy. Good luck sleeping with the ghost tonight." Dianna joked.

-17-

Faith fluffed her thick white comforter and peered upward looking for a ghost before turning off the light. She practically fell asleep before her face sunk into her marshmallow-soft pillow with a smile and a deep sigh. She loved her new life even if she was still getting used to it. But sometime around two am, a whoosh sound near her head woke her up in a panic, like a sheet being snapped to get the wrinkles out. Surely dreaming, she couldn't process that something had glided past her like one of the toy planes she used to fly with her father at the park. *The ghost? A moose? What the ...*

She kicked off the comforter and ran toward the light switch but it threw the thing into a frenzy. It picked up speed, ricocheting into the crown molding, ceiling and walls. Its large scalloped wings looked like a flying garbage bag. She squeaked each time it dove at her even though she was trying to keep quiet.

Faith ran to close all the doors that lead to the other rooms, trapping herself in the room with the brown and black furry creature with beady eyes and fangs that might as well have been the length of toothpicks. She jumped on the couch and pulled the comforter over her head. "This isn't going to get him out of my house." Faith peeked out to see where he was but was afraid to look. Still, it was better to see him than be surprised.

Sweat poured down her face; she must have turned the air conditioner off at some point in the middle of the night in order to hear the kids better. The beady thing must have thought he had found the rainforest, it was so hot. Faith had to think of how to get him out of her house. She grabbed a blanket. "If I can hoist this over him, he'll stop flying." She lunged at him. But the blanket floated in slow motion through the air and the creature's furry face dodged her with every round, flying closer to her each time. Faith screeched and ducked out of the way, hiding from his large wingspan.

"This is ridiculous." She exclaimed. She timed how long it took him to make his lap around the room. Crash. Streaks of slime smeared onto the tops of the walls like a stenciled border. She shuddered. Every time he looped around, she swatted him with the blanket. It took several tries. *Whack.* She knocked him down. "Oh thank God,'" thought Faith. She covered him, but he kept moving. "Stop." She told him. "I'm not trying to hurt you. Just please. Stop. Moving." She thought she could scoop him up in a wastebasket, but the blanket was stuck on something. *His wings? His teeth?* "What is it stuck on?" He made a clicking sound and Faith squeaked. "Stop clicking. You're creeping me out." She pleaded with him.

Once she was able to ignore his noises and movement, she was able to slide cardboard under the basket, and trap him. But the spooky mammal kept flitting around inside while she opened the front door to the porch. She managed to set him down, knock the basket over and run away to look out through the blinds on the closed door. "Well great, how am I supposed to know if he got out? What if he's hurt?" Faith went outside again and tip-toed toward the basket, nudging it with her toe in case he was still in there, but she gained courage to get closer and peek in. He was gone. She clutched her chest and sighed with relief.

Faith turned her computer on and looked up "bats in the house". The information scared her more than the damn bat. "Don't catch it on your own … if you have kids in the house, bats can give them gentle bites that may not wake them … call animal control". She rushed into both kids' rooms and threw on the lights to examine them head to toe for anything unusual. She hadn't thought that anything could have come in and traveled throughout the whole house to the front room. She gasped. *The moose. Antlers. Wingspan. The sheet sound. The ghost. How long did he live in Jenna's room and I never noticed?*

Faith slept the remainder of the morning with the lights on. The first thing in the morning, her father came to inspect the windows and sure enough, she hadn't pulled the storm windows up enough when she pulled down the screens leaving spaces at the tops of the windows. Faith didn't even realize that was a thing to look for, to look in and look up. It would have been something that a protective husband would have taken care of. A pang of loneliness came over her.

The next day Jenna wondered if she'd see the moose again. "No honey. No more moose sightings in your room. And no more ghosts." They both breathed a sigh of relief.

Dianna enjoyed hearing the story while they refilled

their glasses at the restaurant, shaking their heads and laughing until the tears flowed. "I figured I'd be having to get rid of my own spiders. Who knew it would be a freakin' bat?"

"Click, click, click." Dianna tried to creep her out.

Faith shuddered. "Don't you dare. I'm seriously traumatized by it."

"You and me both."

"Want to come see Jenna at dancing school tomorrow?"

"You know I live to see the three year olds dance."

"Liar."

"I'll be there!"

-18-

Dianna met Faith in the waiting area, cradling something in her crossed arms. Faith immediately knew what it was. She put her hands to her chest.

"Here," Dianna sat in the seat Faith cleared for her. "I want Jenna to have this." She handed her the yellow butterfly ballerina.

"Change. Fly. Soar." They whispered together.

"I couldn't possibly."

"I want Jenna to have it. Alicia loved it and I know that Jenna will too."

"Are you sure?"

Dianna nodded.

"She will. I will." Faith stared at her in disbelief.

Dianna reached her arms out and Faith fell into them looking in to the room of prancing girls in pink tights and tutus. Sitting up, she said, "Ah, the beginner ballerinas! I just love that age." She held her heart and stared out for a moment. "I always thought Alicia would dance," Dianna said while watching Jenna leaping with the other girls. "I'm glad Jenna is dancing even though Frank said no. I mean, look at how much fun she's having." They both peeked into the room. Tiny dust particles floating on sunbeams enhanced the beauty of the room; smooth oak accents and touches of soft pink everywhere.

They looked down at Kyle. His low constant hum let them know where he was at all times. He stood and tried walking for the first time. Faith held her breath and fumbled for her phone, sliding the video record button on.

"He's WALKING! Oh my God, put the video on, get him, get him," Dianna instructed. Faith fumbled to hit record on her phone.

"How old is he?" A nosey woman in the waiting area chimed in.

"He's one." Faith lied.

"He's almost two," Dianna corrected.

Faith shot her a look while trying not to add her voiceover to the video.

"He's tiny." The woman said.

"No shit," Dianna leaned to whisper in Faith's ear.

"Shhh," Faith hushed, when out of the corner of her eye, Faith noticed the nosey woman's son. He didn't like that Kyle was getting all the attention. He reached out and stiff-armed him in his forehead, but Kyle kept pushing through. He had his eye on Faith and a smile across his face until he reached her lap.

Tears poured down Faith's face. "Good job!" She fumbled to press "stop" on the video and kissed him all over his face while he giggled contagiously.

"Look at you!" Dianna beamed. "I knew you could do it."

Faith could hardly see through her tears. "He's proving everyone wrong."

"And so are you, Faith." Dianna said. "So are you."

Jenna's class ended in time for her to see Kyle walking all by himself. “Brudder!” She kept the pet name, even though she was able to pronounce it now. “You’re walking. I’m so proud of you.” She twirled; prancing around him and Kyle’s contagious belly laughs filled the room. Faith wiped her eyes for the last time. “He’s going to be okay,” she whispered. “We’re all going to be okay.”

The End.

Resources

Places to Start to Help Your Family with Alcoholism:

The Substance Abuse and Mental Health Services Administration (SAMHSA) https://www.help.org/drug-abuse-hotline "refers callers to mental health and substance abuse resources in their area. All programs recommended by SAMHSA meet federal guidelines for assisting people with mental health and addiction disorders, and all inquiries are kept strictly confidential. 1-800-662-HELP (4357)..."

AA Hotline: 5 Reasons to Call the 24-Hour Number https://alcoholicsanonymous.com/5-reasons-to-call-an-aa-24-hour-hotline/
"If you're struggling with an addiction to alcohol, help is just a phone call away, thanks to the 24-hour AA hotlines. Independently run by Alcoholics Anonymous (AA) groups in cities throughout the world, these AA hotlines provide information and refer callers to volunteers who are ready around the clock to answer questions and offer help. Here are the different ways that calling an AA hotline can help you overcome your alcohol addiction.

1. Call the AA Hotline to Help You Stay Sober
First and foremost, the AA hotline is available for anyone who needs help to stop drinking. Whether you're just starting on your road to recovery or you've been sober for a few years, whenever you need some support, the AA hotline is there for you. When you call the hotline, you'll be connected with an AA member who can talk to you

Resources

about your current situation and help you the best that they can. The AA member you speak with will have been sober for at least a year and working AA's Twelve Step program. They can offer reassurance, practical suggestions, and even take you to an AA meeting near you … Once you reach the last step of the program, you too may help others by answering AA hotline calls. If you're looking for something more than just an AA meeting or support, such as a rehab facility or detox options, call 800-839-1686 to speak with an addiction treatment advisor."

2. Information on Meetings and AA Services
"If you're looking for an AA meeting in your area, call the AA hotline to find information about local meetups, dates and times, and even how the meetings are generally run. If you're out of town for the week and are unsure where the local meeting is held in the city you're in temporarily, someone on the other end of the AA hotline will be able to help…"

3. Treatment Programs for Alcohol Abuse
"The Twelve Traditions of AA make it clear that AA doesn't affiliate with, or endorse, any treatment programs, hospitals, or other institutions that provide services and support to people who want to stop drinking and recover from alcohol addiction. However, AA works in cooperation with these treatment facilities by providing AA support and meetings for people in inpatient and outpatient rehab programs..."

Resources

4. You are a Friend or Family Member of an Alcoholic
"The AA hotline exists to help anyone who is suffering from the effects of drinking, including family members and friends of someone who is abusing alcohol. You might call the hotline because you're looking for ways to help that person stop drinking or maybe you're the one who needs the support. Alcoholism can destroy relationships and AA recognizes that loved ones of alcoholics also need someone to talk to. You may not know how to deal with a loved one's addiction or you may want to help but don't know where to start—this is how the AA hotline can help.
The hotline can offer information on resources for family members of alcohol abusers to help cope with the situation and answer any questions you may have about AA meetings and how you can help your loved one."

5. You're an AA Member Who Has Relapsed
"If you've been attending AA meetings and working on sobriety, it can be hard to admit you've relapsed and are drinking again. But the AA hotline can connect you with an experienced member who can help at any time, day or night. The member can take you to a meeting, or just talk without judgment and help you find your way back to sobriety … Always know that there is help available, whether it be through the AA hotline, or by talking to a treatment advisor…"

Resources

AA Hotline: 24-Hour Availability
"The 24-hour hotlines maintained by Alcoholics Anonymous are available in many communities around the world. In areas not served by a local AA group, AA's toll-free numbers can put anyone concerned about drinking in touch with people who can help. Since there's no such thing as taking a day off from your recovery, the AA hotline also doesn't take a day off. AA members are available to take calls 24 hours a day, so don't be afraid to call in the middle of the night if you're struggling or just need someone to talk to.
Remember that you're speaking to someone who has gone through a similar experience to you and can empathize and will not judge you, regardless of your situation or current mindset.
If you feel like you need more than just the AA hotline, there is also other help available…"

Al-Anon
"Are You Living With an Alcoholic Spouse or Partner?
https://al-anon.org/newcomers/how-can-i-help-my/alcoholic-spouse-or-partner/ Are you involved with someone whose drinking is bothering you? How do you cope with an intimate relationship that is affected by alcoholism? Living with a spouse, partner or significant other who exhibits a drinking problem can have devastating effects on our emotional well-being, our personal relationships, our professional life and sometimes even our physical health. Attending Al-Anon Family Group meetings might provide

Resources

the support and tools needed to deal with the effects of alcoholism on very important relationships."

Al-Anon Meetings Worldwide (including Alateen):
Alateen "is a fellowship of young people (mostly teen-agers) whose lives have been affected by someone else's drinking whether they are in your life drinking or not." https://al-anon.org/al-anon-meetings/worldwide-al-anon-contacts/

Special Needs Parenting Resources:
There are plenty of online resources available for Special Needs Parenting including respite. Please look up "special needs resources near me" to help with your child's specific special needs.

"We all marry our unfinished business." – Terry Real

Acknowledgements

Thank you to my amazing husband, Erick. You have taught me that happiness plus unwaivering and unconditional love is possible. You are truly my biggest cheerleader. Thank you. Forever.

Thank you to my children Kaitlyn, Brendan, and now Daniel, and Abby, for understanding that my eight o'clock hour is sacred writing time. I love you all.

Thank you to my parents for understanding that *embellishment* is part of being an author.

Thank you to Dianna Schriver, Tracy Weed, Karen Gamble, Maria Daversa, and my walking buddy Ursula Hale for your support and encouragement throughout my writing process.

Dianna, when you told me about Alicia, I knew that I wanted to include her as a character in my story. I hope this book inspires you to write all of Alicia's truth in your version; raw, emotional. It will be so helpful for other special needs parents going through the same thing. Hugs.

Lastly, but most importantly, thank you to my Editor, Natalie Bates, for pushing me to go deeper and always believing in me. You have helped make this book a reality! I look forward to working with you again for the sequel!

About the Author

Michelle Spray is an additional needs mom living in Connecticut with her husband and their blended family. She is currently writing a sequel to One Equals Six (Kyle's journey with 22q). Michelle is proud to supply an underlying theme of hope and inspiration in all of her books.

You can find Michelle's other books including children's books about bravery and being "different" on Amazon:
www.amazon.com/author/michellespray
www.michellespray.com
www.bookshelf123.com

Follow Michelle on all socials @SprayBooksEtc

www.ingramcontent.com/pod-product-compliance
Lightning Source LLC
LaVergne TN
LVHW020632100826
845148LV00012B/2158

* 9 7 8 0 5 7 8 9 2 1 0 0 6 *